Louisa Caroline Tuthill

True Manliness

Or the Landscape Gardener

Louisa Caroline Tuthill

True Manliness
Or the Landscape Gardener

ISBN/EAN: 9783337068172

Printed in Europe, USA, Canada, Australia, Japan

Cover: Foto ©Andreas Hilbeck / pixelio.de

More available books at **www.hansebooks.com**

TRUE MANLINESS;

OR,

THE LANDSCAPE GARDENER.

A Book for Boys and Girls.

By MRS. L. C. TUTHILL.

"Conquer difficulties
By daring to attempt them."

BOSTON:
CROSBY AND AINSWORTH.
NEW YORK: OLIVER S. FELT.
1867.

ELECTROTYPED AT THE
BOSTON STEREOTYPE FOUNDRY,
4 SPRING LANE.

CONTENTS.

TRUE MANLINESS.

CHAPTER I.

LITTLE WAINBOW.

BENEATH the brilliant light of a chandelier, suspended over a marble centre-table, sat Mr. and Mrs. Rose.

The bald head of Mr. Rose shone in that light, looking round and smooth as an ostrich egg: yet Mr. Rose was not an old man; he was on the hither side of forty.

The rings and bracelets of Mrs. Rose sparkled with a lustre very pleasing to herself. Mrs. Rose was fond of ornament. She was embroidering a neck-tie of crimson satin with gold-colored silk, for her darling pet, Clarence Rose.

Mr. Rose was poring over the evening paper.

But who comes here? What a funny little person!

Why, it is Master Clarence. There he stands, four feet ten in his morocco pumps. Long-tailed, purple coat, plaid pantaloons, blue waistcoat, frilled shirt-bosom with turquoise studs — nothing wanting but the neck-tie to complete his elegant toilet !

"Mamma, ith my tavat done ?" demanded the boy.

"Not quite, my darling; but it will be in five minutes."

"Now, thath too bad; the pawty beginth at eight," said Clarence, looking at his enamelled watch, "and ith theven minute patht alweady."

Mrs. Rose plied her needle swiftly, and in a few minutes the neck-tie was completed.

"Let me arrange it for you, dear," said Mrs. Rose.

"No, I'll awange it mythelf; you don't know the latht fathonable tie." So saying, he turned towards the large mantel mirror, and making the embroidered ends stand out like Louis Napoleon's mustache, he exclaimed, "Thath the go !" and made a low bow to himself.

"I shall send the carriage for you at eleven," said the delighted, admiring Mrs. Rose, as the boy left the room.

Mr. Rose, meantime, ensconced behind the newspaper, seemed not to notice what was going on; but an occasional hem, or rather more guttural sound, might have betrayed to others, not pre-occupied, that he was fully aware of what was passing.

As soon as the front door had closed upon Clarence, Mr. Rose said, with a very decided emphasis, —

"That boy must be sent to school."

"Send Clarence to school! Why, Mr. Rose, you are not in earnest."

"Never more so in my life," was the calm reply.

"O, husband, that would be cruel to him and to me," said she, with tears in her eyes.

"The cruelty would be in allowing the boy to become a silly, effeminate dandy. Here is an advertisement stating that the Rev. Mr. Warren — by the way, an old classmate of mine at school — will receive four boys into his family, to fit them for college or for mercantile life. He is settled in the village of Raceville, nearly two hundred miles from the city. A railroad passes by the village, and of course it is easy of access. I don't intend to send Clarence to college; his defective speech would prevent that. I hope in the end to take him into my counting-room."

Mrs. Rose was now sobbing violently, with her frilled handkerchief to her eyes.

"Now, my dear, you will take the goffering out of your laced handkerchief. Be reasonable. Clarence must leave home next Monday morning; the term at Mr. Warren's commenced the first of September, a week ago."

"So soon? I can't part with him, indeed I

can't," shrieked Mrs. Rose, almost going into hysterics.

"I am sorry for you, Eliza, but your weak indulgence would ruin the boy, if it has not already done it. I have set down my foot, and there's no *if* nor *but* in the matter. Have him ready to start early on Monday morning. I will write to my old chum this very night. I hope he will be able to make a man of Clarence — weak timber he will have to work upon."

"He is *not* weak in mind, but delicate bodily; he is small of his age," sobbed out Mrs. Rose, hysterically.

"Let me see; he must be thirteen. Goodness! At his age I was clerk in a hardware store — a big strapping fellow able to earn my own living. I'll go and write my letter."

Mrs. Rose, knowing that her husband had fully made up his mind, soon wiped her eyes, and to console herself began to embroider another neck-tie — green silk with a pink figure, which she called an arabesque pattern; or rather it was so termed in the fashion-plate from which she copied the pattern. She had nearly completed her work, when Clarence came home, sleepy, tired, and cross as a bear.

"Come, tell me, darling, something about the party," said she.

"I *won't.* I want to go wight to bed," snarled he.

"I am afraid you haven't had a pleasant evening, my dear."

"They made fun of me, and called me little Wainbow," said Clarence ; and without further ceremony he left the room, Mrs. Rose calling after him, —

"What, not one kiss, when I have sat up working for you till twelve o'clock ! "

CHAPTER II.

GOING, GOING.

THE next morning Clarence was too sick to come down to breakfast. Late hours and late suppers evidently did not agree with the délicate boy.

The tête-à-tête breakfast of Mr. Rose and his wife was as unsocial as possible. Mr. Rose resorted to the morning paper, as he sipped his coffee. Mrs. Rose was in a pouting humor, but was overawed by the unusual silence of her husband, and ventured no remonstrance against the decision of the previous evening. As he left the table he said, —

"My dear, whatever preparations you have to make for Clarence must be completed by next Saturday evening."

Mr. Rose closed the door rather more quickly than usual, and was soon out of hearing.

Mrs. Rose despatched a messenger for a fashionable tailor, and ordered two full suits of clothing for Clarence, to be completed without fail at the time specified.

Clarence came down to dinner looking pale and forlorn. The curls of fair hair which usually adorned his pretty face were now hanging about it " like sea-weed round a clam."

" Parties don't suit you, boy," said Mr. Rose. " You look as weak and puny as a young kitten who hasn't opened its eyes. Why, your own are scarcely open, and are edged with scarlet. This will never do. A change of air will be beneficial. I am going to send you into the country, to school. You must be nearly thirteen."

" I'm quite that," said Clarence, brightening up. " I thould like to go. The boyth poke fun at me, and thay I'm tied to mamma'th apon thing."

Mr. Rose laughed heartily, while his other half gave a deep sigh. She had taught Clarence herself, to spare him · from being ridiculed for his broken English, and now dreaded what he would have to encounter among rough boys.

Mr. Rose hitherto had not interfered, considering Clarence more as his wife's plaything, than as a reasonable human being, for whom he was accountable. His action was now decided and prompt.

Mr. Rose continued : " Clarence, I am going to send you two hundred miles from home, by yourself. Do you think you are manly enough to undertake the journey alone ?"

Clarence hesitated a moment; then, looking at Mrs. Rose in a helpless, sheepish way, he said, in a whining voice, "I wather have mamma go with me."

"No; you must go alone; you wished to be released from a woman's ' apon thing,' and it is true you have been tied there too long. Your tongue, too, has been tied; and you must get it loosened, or you will never do for lawyer, doctor, clergyman, or merchant either. You are to start in the morning train on Monday next for Raceville."

"Can't I go part of the way with the dear boy?" asked Mrs. Rose, with the tears streaming down her cheeks.

"Not a step," was the stern reply.

"Am I to fit for tollege?" asked Clarence.

"If you will mind your R-s and S-es as well as your P-s and Q-s, you may; but I do not think you ever will."

"I thall want loth of thingth and plenty of money," said Clarence.

"You will be amply provided with everything needful. I am ashamed of you, Clarence. When I was of your age I could have entered college, if I had chosen to do so; and was a member of a Debating Society; and you! why, you are a big baby, and ought to wear corals and a silver whistle about your neck, instead of that flashy cravat."

"My tavat is a puffet beauty; everybody thaid tho, latht night."

" Listen to me, Clarence," said Mr. Rose, angrily. " I have written to Mr. Warren my wishes concerning you, and prepared him for what would have otherwise been a surprise to him. One thing more I have to say to you. I shall not take the least notice of any complaint you may make about your master or your schoolmates. You are to be absent one year — so you need not ask to come home till the next September."

" Not if he should be homesick?" suggested Mrs. Rose, dolorously.

" He must not be homesick. He must be brave. When boys go in to swim early in the spring, when the water is very cold, they plunge in boldly, and shiver at first; but soon they don't mind it; they grow warm. So it must be with you, Clarence: plunge into school boldly, and you will soon get used to it."

Mrs. Rose was an habitual weeper. She was now crying immoderately.

" Don't ki, mamma. I thant be hometick," said Clarence.

" Ridiculous! Absurd!" exclaimed Mr. Rose. " You see, my dear, the absolute necessity of sending the boy away. I am glad to find that he shows more willingness to go than I expected. You must not weaken his resolution."

CHAPTER III.

GONE !

MONDAY morning. It was a glorious September day, bland and bright; a few red leaves on the maples, a few yellow elm leaves quietly falling to mother earth.

Mr. Rose drove with Clarence to the station, and placed him in the car which would take him all the way to Raceville.

At the earnest request of Mr. Rose, his wife did not come down to breakfast that morning; so there was no leave taking on her part. Stern as Mr. Rose seemed, his voice trembled and his eyes moistened as he said, " God bless you," to the boy, who was leaving the shelter of his roof, utterly unprepared for hardship of any kind.

Clarence deposited the checks for two trunks and one box in his green silk purse, — through the meshes of which glittered several gold pieces, — and stuck his ticket under the gold band of his blue velvet cap.

The novelty of a journey by himself, but still more the possession of two *brand-new* trunks, filled with beautiful clothing, and that square box, with its cake, candies, and other toothsome dainties, quite reconciled the boy to parting with home. He nodded to Mr. Rose from the window of the car, with a satisfied smile, as the car started, and waved his hand with a flourish, that meant, "I can take care of myself."

At this moment a young lady took a seat beside him. She had in her arms a small white and tan dog, which she soon carefully accommodated on her lap.

The train whizzed and tore on, and soon "miles and *mileses*" were between Clarence and his city home.

Soon his attention was drawn to the lady and her pretty, dumb companion. And it was not strange, for they were both worthy of notice.

The lady apparently had seen but eighteen summers — eighteen pleasant ones, judging by her bright, intelligent face. Her dark gray eyes were so sparkling that her other features were scarcely noticed; they were not remarkably handsome, but those splendid eyes and the beautiful glow of health on her plump cheeks rendered her face charmingly attractive.

The little dog, with its long silken ears of a bright, tan color, lay quietly in her lap, and seemed to listen to the caressing remarks of a voice not "low," but "sweet."

"What ith your dogth's name?" asked Clarence.

"He rejoices in the name of Winfield, but we call

him, for brevity, Win, and sometimes Winny; and pardon me for making the same inquiry of yourself. What is your name?"

"Clanth Wothe," was the reply.

"May I take the further liberty to inquire how far you intend travelling to-day, Mr. Wothe?"

"I am going to Watheville," replied Clarence, coloring deeply at the consciousness of his defective speech.

"Watheville! I do not know any place of that name on this route. How far is it from the city?"

"Two hunded mileth."

"That is just as far as I am going. I shall be glad of your escort."

The lady chatted away to her dog, in a babytalk, that Clarence suspected was an imitation of his own; and he kept silence, excepting as he answered the questions from time to time addressed to him.

"Win, wake up! oo lathy itty dog," said the *fast* young lady. "Look at this pretty young genty."

The creature turned its dark eyes with such a fearfully human look at Clarence that he was quite startled, and said, —

"He theems to know what you thay to him."

"Indeed he does. I wish he could talk. I can teach him everything else," said she, pulling Win's long ears.

"You ought to thend him wha I'm going," said Clarence.

" Where is that?"

" To cool," replied Clarence, in a loud tone.

" He's cool enough now. When the weather was warm, I did send him to a cool place, for fear he would go mad. You would be cooler if you took off your overcoat."

Clarence was so vexed at being thus misunderstood, that when the train stopped at the next station, he changed his seat, and regaled himself with a lunch of sandwiches and cakes, placed for him, by his indulgent mamma, in the capacious pocket of his overcoat.

After a while he began to feel quite solitary, in the midst of so many entire strangers, and now and then brushed a tear from his blue eyes. The purse and its contents were, however, an unfailing source of relief. He took it frequently from his pocket, and held it up to admire the "shiners" within, and carefully replaced it in his inner coat pocket.

When the train stopped for dinner, Clarence, contrary to the command of Mr. Rose, got out of the car, and went to the table. Why shouldn't he dine, like other folks, even if he had eaten a lunch? So he hurried down his dinner like "other folks," paid his half dollar, and dropped his purse into the pocket of his overcoat.

After dinner, Raceville seemed to the solitary boy a kind of Cape Flyaway. Every time the conductor came along, the boy asked if they had almost reached Watheville.

He began to be very sick, — the motion of the train not agreeing with an overloaded stomach, — and he was obliged frequently to put his head out of the window.

He began to cry right heartily. Just then the conductor called out Raceville, and tapped Clarence on the shoulder.

Gladly Clarence rushed out of the car, and soon spied his trunks and box on the platform.

" Any baggage, mister," said a porter.

" Want a carriage, sir," bawled another.

" Yith, I want a cawedge; an I've got two twunks and a both."

The men winked at each other, and the hackdriver asked for his checks.

Clarence felt for his purse, in this pocket and that, — in every pocket, — and it was not to be found.

" How do I know them is your twunks, if you can't show the checks?" said the hackman.

" Betause I know it," was the angry answer. " Take 'em up and put 'em on the cawedge." .

A provoking laugh followed, and the inquiry, —

" Where are you going?"

" To Mitht Wawnth cool."

" There isn't a person of that name in all Raceville. You must be a runaway," said the porter, " or else you've mistaken the place."

2

"I am not a wunaway; I am the son of Mithter Wothe, of New Yawk; he put me on the twain himthelf."

"That he did, indade," said a well-dressed Irishman, handing out three checks. "Take up the young masther's luggage, and don't stand here insulting him."

"Why, Pat, how came you here?" exclaimed Clarence, astonished to see the waiter from his own home.

"The misthress sent me to take care of you, but not to let you see me unless you got into throuble."

"But how did you find my puth!" said Clarence, seizing the purse.

"Afther you had dined, like a gintleman, and was getting into the car, I took it out of your pocket, for fear some one else would do it; for I saw a little paper with, 'Look out for pickpockets,' on it, posted up at the station; so I just thought I should be the most convanient pickpocket for you."

"Don't tell papa of that," said Clarence; "he might not be pleased with you."

Pat laughed, and said, "Better pleased that I should do it, than that you should have lost checks, money, and all."

The carriage soon conveyed them to the parsonage, the residence of the Rev. Albertus Warren.

As Pat assisted the waiter at the parsonage to

carry the trunks to the room appropriated to Clarence, he offered the man a five-dollar gold piece, saying, " The misthress sent this to you, begging you would be kind to her darlint, Masther Clarence. She would pick out her two eyes for him."

Honest Tom refused the money.

" Now, that's a mysthery Father Malony himself couldn't explain. I thought all Yankees loved money."

" They like to earn their money fairly, and not be paid till they have earned it. Mr. Warren does not allow us to take money from the boys. I'll be as kind to the popinjay as I can be, though he looks mighty proud."

" He's a mighty nice lad," said Pat, warmly, " only ," he added in a low tone, " a leetle bit spoilt."

While this conversation was going on in the long entry, Clarence was being kindly received by Mr. Warren.

" This lady you have seen before," said Mr. Warren, as he presented Mrs. Warren.

Clarence was surprised and embarrassed when he saw that it was the lady whom he had abruptly left in the car.

She smiled roguishly, but greeted him warmly. She had walked from the station, and reached the parsonage long enough before Clarence to tell Mr. Warren of her meeting the boy, and of her perplexity about "Watheville," and about going to "cool."

"I will show you to your room, Clarence," said Mr. Warren, kindly. "We shall have tea in half an hour. And, my lad, I shall ask you no questions at table, for Mr. Rose informs me that you have a defect in your speech, which, however, we hope, in time, entirely to cure."

CHAPTER IV.

THE "COOL."

WHEN the bell rang for tea, the family, consisting of Mr. and Mrs. Warren, Jack Jimson, and Stackpole Clap, came to the table; but Clarence did not make his appearance.

"I will go for the stranger as soon as I have poured out your tea," said Mrs. Warren. She tapped gently at the door of the room assigned to Clarence. No voice bade her come in. She opened the door. The poor boy had thrown himself upon the bed, and cried himself to sleep. Mrs. Warren did not disturb him. She closed the door quietly, and went down stairs.

About an hour after she went again, and, awakening him, begged him to come down stairs and take supper.

Clarence roused himself, and Mrs. Warren, seeing his hair was in wild disorder, with one of her
own small side combs arranged the fair curls about
his face, just as she would if he had been a pretty
baby. This was not just the thing for Clarence,
who had had too much petting already; and so
Mr. Warren said to his wife, after she had kindly
and tenderly devoted herself to him, while the boy
partook of the nice, warm supper set before him.

Mr. Warren took her aside, and said, " This will
never do. The boy must be turned in with the
others at once. I am afraid he will receive rather
rough treatment, but he might as well go through
with it first as last."

" Spare him for a week, at least," pleaded his
young wife.

" No, I have decided otherwise. You must not
indulge him, because he is a spoiled pet. I shall
take him to the library, and make him acquainted
with Jack and Stackpole."

" But he is tired and sleepy," still urged Mrs.
Warren.

" Please, my dear, not another word in his
behalf."

Mr. Warren then returned to Clarence, and said,
" The boys pass an hour together every night in
the library, and amuse themselves according to
their own pleasure. I will make you acquainted
with them."

They found the two boys engaged in playing a game of checkers.

Jack Jimson was nearly six feet tall. His arms were long in proportion to his body, and his hands immensely large. His coarse black hair stood up as stiffly as the bristles of a ‧shoe brush, and his large ears were a deeper red than his face, which was by no means destitute of color. His wide mouth displayed a set of strong yellow teeth, which had not been subjected to a dentist's manipulations, ‧judging from their remarkable irregularity.

He rose from his seat, and bowed awkwardly to Clarence, looking down upon him as though he had been a squirrel or a canary bird.

Stackpole Clap was not much larger than Clarence. He might possibly have boasted of full five feet of height, but seemed not as tall, from an habitual stoop, which might have been acquired from perpetual cringing. He walked as if he were always saying to the very ground, "By your leave;" not because he was humble and modest, but because he was obsequious, and had not independence enough to say either his body or his soul was his own. His hair, straight as a candle, was almost as white, and his pale-blue eyes wandered even when he spoke, as though seeking for approbation from those about him. He bowed low to‐ Clarence, looking at the same time at Jack.

Clarence felt exceedingly shy and embarrassed.

Jack Jimson assumed an air of immense superiority, and eyed the new comer as he would a cat which he intended to torment, his staring dark eyes and heavy eyebrows giving him the air of a young bandit.

Poor little Clarence shrunk from the saucy stare, and fairly trembled when Jack asked, in a coarse voice, —

" Mister, what — may — I — call you? "

" Wothe," meekly replied Clarence.

""Well, Wothe, you got seasick and homesick on the railroad; didn't you? "

" Yith, thir."

A loud laugh from Jack, echoed by Stackpole Clap, sounded through the apartment.

Clarence, unaccustomed to such violent impertinence, roused himself, and said to Stackpole, —

" You might be mo' polite to a — a " — Clarence hesitated; he could not say *stranger* — " new acquaintanth."

Stackpole stifled his laughter, and pretended to sneeze.

" Why! how now! There's some spunk in you. More, I dare say, than there is in my toady, if you are such a dolly-boy."

Clarence took no notice of the remark, but turned over the leaves of a book, and commenced reading to himself.

The other boys resumed the game that had been

interrupted; but that was soon ended by Jack's gaining the victory.

"Well, now, Jack, tell us one of your funny stories," said Stackpole.

"Willingly," was the reply, "if Mr. Wothe has no objection."

"Thertainly I have not."

"I suppose you have always lived in the city. Do you know much about the country?"

"I do not."

"Well, once upon a time," said Jack, "not very long ago, a great, horrid black bear prowled about this very house. He came out of the woods, not far off, as hungry as hungry could be, all ready to eat up somebody. He was an awful big creature, a great deal bigger than an ox, with teeth as long as my forefinger, and a mouth big enough to take your head right off, Mr. Wothe, at a single mouthful. Well, there was a small boy at this school, about your size, with just such curly hair and blue eyes; a real dolly-boy, mamma's pet,—a pretty creature, just fit to put in a toy-shop window, to please little eight-year-old girls. Well, that pretty boy put his head out that window, one night, when he heard the bear growl; and, lo and behold, the bear was prowling about just here, and when he saw that curly head, he snapped at it, and scalped the boy entirely; took the skin right off the top of his head, curls and all, as neatly as a

Pottawatamie Indian could have done it with his tomahawk. Never a single hair grew again on the top of that sweet boy's head."

Stackpole giggled and snickered. Jack turned fiercely upon him, and said, " None of your laughing, just as I am coming to the tragical end."

Stackpole collapsed. Jack went on.

" Well, one day, a whole month after, when his head had healed over, the boy — let's see — Pink — yes, that was his name — went to the woods with some other boys, a nutting. Suddenly they heard a tremendous growl, and all ran. Poor Pink was so frightened that he tumbled down ; and the bear, having had a taste of the delicate little dolly-boy before, liked it well, and devoured him now entirely. Nothing remained of him but a few gilt buttons and a beautiful red neck-tie.

" What do you think of that, Mr. Wothe ? "

" I think the black ba' wath much like youthelf," said Clarence, who had completely recovered self-possession.

Stackpole, in spite of himself, and his fear of Jack, laughed outright.

Jack seized the toady by the shoulder, and gave him a shaking so violent that the boy shrieked, and the noise brought Mr. Warren to the library.

" How now ! " he exclaimed ; " what does this mean ? Jack and Stackpole fighting ? "

Neither of the combatants answered.

"He," said Clarence, pointing to Jack, "told a funny thowy, and that boy laughed at it; then *he* thook him."

"Jack, you are violent in your demonstrations; ask Stackpole's pardon."

"Pardon, Pole," muttered Jack.

"It is granted, entirely," replied Stackpole, bowing in the most cringing manner to big Jack.

"I am sorry," added Mr. Warren, "that our young friend Clarence should have witnessed such behavior, the very first evening of his arrival."

"O, it wath funny," said Clarence, laughing. "It hath done me good."

And so it had. Though petted, and rendered effeminate by weak indulgence, Clarence was, naturally, neither silly nor a coward. He had been very little in company with boys of his own age, but had been much with older people, and was not habitually bashful.

Mr. Warren now summoned the boys to the parlor for evening prayers.

CHAPTER V.

ROLLING THE R.

At the very outset of his school course, Clarence had thus rendered Jack Jimson, the bully of the school, his formidable enemy.

In addition to the four boarders in Mr. Warren's family, there were eight or ten boys from the village, who attended as day-scholars. Over all these Jack ruled by strength of fist, and no one had yet dared to brave the strong despot. The small boys looked up to him as young Indians do to their savage chief, and the larger ones durst not measure their strength with his, either singly or combined.

Mr. Warren, though a kind man, and an excellent teacher, knew little of the *morale* of the school, excepting intellectually. As long as they conducted themselves properly in his presence, and gave good recitations, he was satisfied, and made no further investigations.

Not so with his "fast" young wife. She knew much more of what was going on out of school. She was better acquainted with the boys, and, with a woman's quick intuition, understood their characters much more thoroughly than did her husband, with all his learning — his mathematics, Greek and Latin. She knew what elements made up the character of Jack Jimson, as well as she knew the contents of the castors on her dinner-table. If she had made the comparison between them, she would have said that mustard, red pepper, and vinegar were constituent elements in the composition of Jack Jimson's character, while the oil predominated in that of Stackpole Clap. She had already learned that Clarence was not a soft custard. He had ruled Mrs. Rose at home; he had ruled the servants, and apparently Mr. Rose. It was a surprise to the boy when Mr. Rose "set down his foot," and ordered Clarence off to school, who thought himself master of the house.

Clarence had not yet been allowed to go into the school-room with the other boys, though he had now been at Raceville a whole week: neither had he been allowed again to pass the hour of evening recreation in the library.

And what was he doing all that time? Learning to speak his own name with Mrs. Warren. Again to be taught by a woman! This was a bitter pill, but nicely sugared over by kindness.

"Clarence," said she, "I want to save you from ridicule. Jack Jimson is ready to break out in his coarse haw, haw, haw! every time you open your lips."

"I don't mind Jack Jimthon, *that*," said Clarence, snapping his delicate white finger and thumb.

"But you must mind *me*. I do not wish to have you ridiculous, and you make yourself so by your baby-talk. You must learn to speak your own name, *Rose*;" and little Mrs. Warren *rolled* the *R* like a Bourdeaux Frenchman.

"Thwothe," said Clarence.

Over and over again the persistent teacher repeated the word from day to day; but finding her pupil made little progress, she tried the. simpler word *rat*. Her perseverance was rewarded; for at the end of the week, her pupil, who had made a tremendous effort, had at last succeeded in *rolling* the *R* — to him the first step on the mountain Difficulty.

———◆———

CHAPTER VI.

HARVEY AMADORE.

ALTHOUGH Mrs. Warren had kept Clarence from the school-room, and had asked him as few questions as possible at table, through the mimicry of Jack Jimson he had become an object of curiosity and of ridicule to every boy in the school. His sobriquet on the playground was "Clanthe Wothe, the dolly-boy."

At the end of the week another boarder arrived, whom Mr. Warren introduced at the tea-table as Harvey Amadore. A right pleasant face had Harvey Amadore. His hazel eyes were just the color of his wavy hair, and his clear, ruddy complexion betokened perfect health. His large mouth, which was seldom entirely closed, displayed a set of clean, handsome teeth, and his broad chin and ample forehead added a strongly intellectual character to a countenance strikingly expressive of great humor and a genial disposition. With all her penetration, Mrs. Warren felt there was something about this new boy that, at the first glance, she did not understand.

Clarence was glad that the new-comer's seat was on his side of the table, and drew from it the pleasing inference that he would be on his side in more ways than one.

The next day was Sunday. The boys sat in the pew with Mrs. Warren, directly in front of the pulpit. Harvey brought his own prayer-book, much worn, but apparently carefully preserved, for it was covered with calico. This amused the two boys at the end of the pew, and induced Clarence to make the comparison between that and his own new prayer-book, with its purple velvet binding and gilt clasps.

While Harvey Amadore was intently listening, and devoutly responding to the Litany, Jack and

Stackpole were holding a whispered consultation, the result of which was, a piece of tobacco placed upon Harvey's prayer-book. Harvey shook it off indignantly. He had scarcely recovered from the shock induced by this irreverent interruption, when a piece of candy was placed upon his prayer-book by Clarence, his neighbor on the other side. He returned it, and whispered to Clarence, "Please don't trouble me."

It was some time before Harvey could compose his mind, and bring back his wandering thoughts. He listened to the sermon, however, with great interest, in spite of the restlessness of his right hand neighbors, and the loud breathing of Clarence, who was taking a comfortable nap. Mrs. Warren was afraid to awaken him, lest he should speak out and disturb her good husband.

On the way home, Harvey and Clarence walked together. The former was dressed in a suit of stout gray cloth, and Clarence contrasted his own fine clothing with that of his companion with great satisfaction.

Clarence was perfumed with otto of roses, musk, and mille-fleurs. The perfume had been sickening to Harvey in church, and now, even in the open air, it was offensive to his olfactory nerves.

"You are fond of perfumes, I perceive," said Harvey. "Musk is particularly disagreeable to me."

"Ith it? Then I won't uthe it any mo'," replied Clarence.

"You are very kind," said Harvey.

"I thould like to be kind to thomething, even a *rat.*"

This was said with such startling emphasis on the last word, that Harvey, surprised and much amused, looked eagerly into the face of his companion. The expression was not silly, and it was kindly.

"You did not mean to call *me* a rat? I hope we shall be good friends," said Harvey; "but don't offer me candy in church; it disturbs me. Not so much, however, as tobacco — odious, disgusting tobacco."

"We' not allowed to chew tobacco aw to thmoke thegars here," said Clarence; "*they* do, both," — turning his head around, to see if the other boys were near.

They were some distance behind.

"Well, *we* will try to keep the rules of the school. I am for obedience to authority. We shall be a great deal happier if we try to do right. We must help each other."

"How old be you?" asked Clarence.

"I am fourteen."

"I am thirteen." A bright color flushed his face, and the boy, delighted that he had overcome one difficulty, repeated, with exultation, "THIRTEEN."

They had now arrived at the gate of the parsonage.

Jack and Stackpole, as they walked home together, were discussing the new scholar.

"He looks as if he might be a right jolly fellow," said Jack; "but he don't act like one."

"Why not?" asked the toady, Stackpole Clap.

"He threw off the *cud* of tobacco as if it had been a rattlesnake. Then he was so awful devout. We will smoke out the young hypocrite. I'll warrant you he expects to recommend himself to Mrs. Warren and her deary by his pious ways at church. But we'll make him show another face. No hypocrites for me."

"Nor for me, either," responded Stackpole.

"As for dolly-boy, we shall have fun enough with him to-morrow, for he is going to join our class in school. Think of that! *Our* class of big boys. We'll hustle him."

"So we will. *Our* class? Who would have thought it? *We'll hustle him,*" said Toady.

"Come, we must hurry on. I shouldn't wonder, now, if the new boy should take a fancy to that fine-as-a-fiddle boy, just because he is so much better dressed than himself. They are, excepting on the outside, animals of the same sort, — soft, soft, — don't you think so?"

"Yes, I do indeed," was the quick reply; "very soft."

3

"Well, now, on second thoughts, I don't think so. They are no more alike than a pea and a pumpkin."

"Ain't they? So they ain't!" muttered Toady, who was fairly caught, and had to whiffle round like a weathercock in a high wind.

Foolish, wicked boys, thus to spend the blessed hours of the Lord's day.

CHAPTER VII.

MISCHIEF BREWING.

Letter from Clarence Rose to Mrs. Rose : —

RACEVILLE, September 20, 18—.

DEAR MAMMA : I can say Rat. I can say Rose. Mr. Warren had the dentist to examine my teeth, and the surgeon to look at my throat, palate, &c. They said they were all right, and nothing prevented my speaking like other boys, if I would only try. Mrs. Warren has taken great pains with me, and rolled her tongue for a whole week to teach me how to speak. I thought I should tie my tongue into a knot, I tried so hard to roll the R; but I finally succeeded. Wasn't it kind in Mrs. Warren to keep me out of school till I did? I don't cry, now, after I am in bed at night, as I did when I first came here — only now and then.

I am in school with the other boys now. You ought to see what a nice school-room we have ; it is carpeted with a pretty green and brown carpet, and the desks are of black walnut, covered with green cloth. All round the room are hung maps and pictures. The windows look out on a garden, which has in it dahlias, tuberoses, china-asters, and several other flowers in bloom.

The school-room is in one wing of the building, and in the other wing, to match, are our bed-rooms, four of them, all on the first floor. It seems as though these two wings had been added to the par-sonage just for us boys.

I thank you, dear mamma, for teaching me to write and to spell. We don't spell out, but write on our slates the words, just as I used to at home. Every spelling lesson of mine has been O. K. Mine was the only slate that had no mistake. I thought how much pains you had taken with my spelling and definitions.

My box of cakes, candies, and sweetmeats was quite forgotten, till, the other night, I asked Mrs. Warren for it. I told her what was in it, and she said I had better make a feast for the boys in the school-room, than to go by myself and " guzzle down goodies like a glutton." Wasn't that funny? She *is* very funny. So we knocked open the box, and O, what lots of goodies !

We had a jolly time in the library — I, and Jack, and Stackpole, and the new boy. Thomas, the waiter, brought in saucers, spoons, &c. I carried a saucer of your nice strawberry preserves, and some of your pound-cakes, to Mrs. Warren. I did not make myself sick, and I never enjoyed myself more in all my life. The boys thought it was to celebrate the arrival of Harvey Amadore, the new boy. Do you know the Amadores? The boys call him a Trojan. He wears plain gray clothes, but I think they were made by a fashionable tailor, they fit so nicely. I am in the same class with him in English studies. We have ten day-scholars in our school; and Jack Jimson is the bully of the school. I don't like Stackpole Clap; he sniggers, and winks at Jack, every time I speak. He is as mean as dirt, and as dirty as mean.

Tell papa I can say Rat and Rose, and give my love to him. I think he did well to send me here. I hope you don't feel lonely. I don't like to be laughed at; do you, dear mamma? I wonder why the boys call me dolly-boy. They never did in New York; though at the party they did call me little Wainbow. Dolly, or not dolly, I am

Your affectionate son,
CLARENCE ROSE.

P. S. Tell Pat I haven't forgot how nicely he picked my pocket. Whenever I see my purse, I think of him, with many thanks.

The new boy, Harvey Amadore, was already far advanced in Latin and Greek, and was really enjoying Cicero and Xenophon; but his English studies had been much neglected. Clarence had the laugh at Harvey when he saw, in one of his exercises, women spelt *wimmen*, and candidate spelt *kandydait*.

"We won't laugh at each other," said Harvey. "I will **try** to correct my spelling, and you your pronunciation. We will help each other."

"Agreed. There, I thaid agreed," said Clarence, exultingly.

On the play-ground, one day, Jack Jimson called Harvey Amadore aside, and said, —

"I wonder how you can be so intimate with that silly little monkey — Wothy Pothy, as we call him. You might be one of *us*, if you chose."

"And what are you?" asked Harvey, with a smile.

"Jolly boys, every one," replied Jack, drawing up his tall, thin person, and holding his arms akimbo.

"None are merrier than I," said Harvey.

"That's the mischief of it. You can play shinney and football with the best of us, and beat us, too; but somehow you don't seem to be of us. We have rare sport with some of the day-scholars. They tell us all that is going on in the village. There is a queer old lady, living all by herself, who has some fine turkeys all ready for market. We are going to borrow one, and roast it in the woods, to-night. We shall have a glorious time. Will you go with us?"

Harvey could scarcely wait till Jack finished speaking; then he burst forth, vehemently, "Steal a turkey! Break the eighth commandment! I am astonished!"

"O, you are a green one! We have taken a chicken once, and eggs again and again; and old Debby has never missed them."

"But you have enough to eat, surely, at Mr. Warren's."

"Well, yes; but it's the fun of the thing, and having a good time in the woods. Now, you won't be so mean as to tell Mr. Warren, Harvey Amadore?"

"I think it would be my duty to do so," was the quick reply.

"Woe to all telltales! The whole school would turn against you, and you would have no peace of your life," said Jack.

"But," said Harvey, "if you break into the woman's house, it will be burglary, as well as theft."

"No, it won't be either. The turkeys are in a shed, back of the house; and we mean to pay the old soul for them some time or other."

After a few moments' hesitation, Harvey said he would not tell Mr. Warren.

" Nor dolly-boy, either?"

" If you mean Clarence Rose, I will not tell him of your wicked intention. I should be sorry to have him know that such bad things could be done by any of his schoolmates."

" You set up for a preacher; do you? A thresh-ing would do you good. I have half a mind to give it to you now;" and, suiting the action to the word, Jack doubled up his big fist and shook it before Harvey's face.

Harvey was a stout, muscular boy, accustomed to gymnastics and other athletic exercises, and of a quick temper. Sudden as a flash, he seized Jack by the waist, tripped him up, and the tall fellow lay sprawling on the ground.

The partisans of Jack, knowing his object in having a private talk with Harvey, had been watch-ing at a distance, anxious to know what would be the result. Great was their astonishment to see their leader, the bully of the school, laid prostrate on the ground. All the boys rushed to the scene of action, and as soon as Jack was on his feet, they cried, " At him, Jack — give it to him, right and left!" Jack squared off to give Harvey a blow. " ' Strike, but hear me,' as said one of the old philosophers," said Harvey, now perfectly cool and self-collected. Another person had witnessed the encounter, and now stepped between the combatants.

" How is this!" exclaimed Mr. Warren.

" Fighting on the play-ground! Harvey Amadore, why did you throw John Jimson to the ground? I had hoped better things of you."

" He insulted and threatened me," replied Harvey; " and I let temper get the better of me, and threw him down."

" And, Jimson, how did you provoke the attack?" Jack was sullen and silent.

" Answer me at. once," said Mr. Warren. " How did you provoke Harvey?"

" I was saucy to him, and threatened to give him a threshing," blurted out the bully.

" Well, then, beg Harvey's pardon, at once," said the master.

" He ought to beg mine," said Jack, pouting his big lips.

" You were the first offender; you ought to make the first acknowledgment," replied Mr. Warren, decidedly.

" Mr. Amadore, I beg your pardon, and grant your grace, &c., &c.," said Jack.

" I am sorry and ashamed to have been so hasty and so angry. I trust you'll forgive me, Jack, and you, too, Mr. Warren. I have a fiery temper, not always under my control," said Harvey, whose anger had passed like a falling star, leaving no trace behind.

Mr. Warren regarded the frank countenance of the noble boy with admiration, and said, —

"I hope you will learn to control your temper, Harvey; and you, Jack Jimson, never say a saucy word to Harvey again, or threaten any one on the play-ground. I must have peace and brotherly kindness among my boys. Remember, Harvey, 'He that ruleth his spirit is greater than he that taketh a city.'"

CHAPTER VIII.

THE BLACK BEAR.

HARVEY AMADORE was troubled in conscience. Ought he to allow the boys to commit the threatened theft? Whom should he consult? He had promised not to tell Mr. Warren.

He at last resolved to learn where Debby lived, and tell her not to put her turkeys where they could be purloined.

At tea time the evening after the scuffle in the play-ground, Mr. Warren was absent. Mrs. Warren said he had gone to pass the night with a clerical friend in a neighboring village.

The boys, as usual, staid some time with Mrs. Warren after tea, and then, as they were about to leave for the library, she said to Harvey, "I will give you a spelling lesson this evening, if you prefer it to any other amusement."

"Thank you," said Harvey; "I do prefer it to anything else I could do just now; for Mr. Warren says I must not study Greek or Latin till I can spell my own language correctly."

As soon as the other boys had left the room, Mrs. Warren commenced the spelling lesson.

"Spell *turkey*," said she.

"Turky."

"No — turkey. Form the plural now."

"Turkies."

"No — turkeys. Now spell *Debby*."

Harvey opened wide his large hazel eyes. Mrs. Warren laughed merrily, and said, "Now spell *thieves*."

Harvey was too much surprised to spell, and Mrs. Warren said, "I will come directly to the point. I walked with my husband to the station this afternoon. On my return, I was fatigued, and sat down to rest on a large stone by the wayside. There was a high board-fence behind me, which enclosed the grounds of a farmer, who sends his son to our school. I immediately recognized the voice of Jack Jimson, who was consulting about a raid upon Debby Hobbs's turkeys. She lives just by the Monkton woods, and the time appointed for their wicked spree was eleven o'clock to-night. Now tell me frankly all you know about it, Harvey. From what I could learn, Jack was afraid Harvey Amadore would betray them, and having learned that Mr. Warren would be absent to-night, he thought it best to hurry matters to a conclusion."

"I know very little more about their plan than you do. It was my intention to warn the woman to take good care of her turkeys; but I am too late for that. They intend to have a barbecue in the woods — to roast the turkey. I doubt if they would be able to eat it, unless they like smoked turkey," said Harvey, laughing.

"We will catch them!" exclaimed young Mrs. Warren, clapping her small hands with real girlish glee. "My plan is this. After the boys have gone to bed, or pretended to go, I will walk down to Debby's with Clarence Rose. Find an opportunity to send him to me before he goes to his room. You must watch for their leaving, and soon after go with Thomas to the woods. I will instruct Thomas just what to do, and you will follow his directions. Meantime, you must be careful not to excite suspicion when you join Jack and Stackpole in the library. Go, now; you have had your spelling lesson."

It was the first week in October. The evening was cool, but not a cloud veiled the bright hemisphere. The silver moon — "sweet regent of the sky" — followed the king of day to his western retreat, leaving night to be ruled by the glittering stars. Mrs. Warren and Clarence, about nine o'clock, went to Debby's cottage.

Harvey sat by the one window of his small room, intently listening for the first movement of Jack Jimson, whose room was next to his own. The part of the house occupied by the boys had been added to the main building; it was a single story, and the windows were only about half a dozen feet from the ground.

About half past ten o'clock two windows were carefully opened, and two boys sprang out of them, and scampered away as if for dear life. Stackpole joined the fire-makers, while Jack made his way to Debby's cottage.

"Don't make a breath of noise," whispered Jack to his companion, the farmer's boy, as they approached the cottage.

The shed in which the lone woman kept her turkeys, when they were ready for market, was only a few steps from the kitchen door, and directly opposite.

Slyly, noiselessly, glided Jack into the shed, and reaching up seized a turkey by the neck. Suddenly his feet were caught in a slip-noose of rope, and a strong pull from the three in the kitchen brought him at full length into the cottage, the turkey still in hand.

Debby was a strong, masculine-looking woman. With the end of the rope she gave Jack several severe whacks across his shoulders.

He shrieked, and let the turkey slip from his hand.

"Now you may go, wicked boy that you are,"

said Debby, while Mrs. Warren and Clarence laughed heartily.

"Go. I see now who has stolen my chicken and eggs, and pay for them you must and shall," cried she, furiously.

Jack tried to rise, but the rope was still about his feet.

"Don't you feel mean," continued Debby, as he tried to extricate himself, "great, big, unmannerly, lubberly boy?"

"I'll pay you, I'll pay you; let me go," cried Jack.

"Let me see. Eggs, sixty cents for three score; chicken, forty cents — just one dollar. Pay me and you may go."

"I haven't the money with me," whimpered the bully.

"I'll lend it to you," said Clarence, taking a bright dollar from his green purse.

"That's right, Clarence," said Mrs. Warren. "Now, Jack, we'll go home."

"Mayn't I go and speak to the other boys?" asked Jack, dolorously.

"No. I prefer to have your company," said Mrs. Warren; and the three, bidding Debby "good night," left the cottage together.

About a quarter of an hour after Jack and Stackpole had started on their mischievous expedition, Thomas, a steady, honest servant, much relied upon by Mr. Warren, tapped at the window where Harvey was on the *qui vive.*

" What is that across your shoulders," asked
Harvey, as he joined Thomas.

" Why, it's a big buffalo skin we used on our
sleigh last winter," was the reply.

" What are you going to do with it, Thomas?"
eagerly asked Harvey.

" You will see when we get near them. young
scamps. We must go very softly, and keep well
behind the trees, till we come near their camp."

As they approached the wood, Thomas said, " I
see a smoke rising. They'll have tough work to
get up a roasting fire. But they really have got up
a blaze," continued he, in a whisper, as they came
near the spot where Stackpole and a half dozen
other boys were piling dry branches upon a fire,
which crackled and sent forth a fitful flame.

" Now's the time. Stand behind that big tree,
Master Harvey."

So saying, Tom spread the big buffalo skin over
himself, and dropped upon all fours. Then he
crept softly along till he came near the group about
the fire, when he set up a tremendous growl. The
boys turned towards the place from which the
ominous sound proceeded, and there, by the light
of the fire, they beheld, as they thought, a big
black bear.

The guilty are cowardly. What a scampering
and shrieking! Some ran one way and some
another. The bear pursued Stackpole, growling

fearfully, till the boy stumbled and fell. Just as the bear reached him, and was sniffing about his head, a voice cried, "Mithter Bear, don't take off hith thealp; pay don't!"

Mrs. Warren, Jack, and Clarence had just arrived to witness the scene.

Stackpole was too much frightened even to recognize the lisping voice of Clarence. He verily believed it was the horrible bear that Jack had described.

Thomas threw off the buffalo-skin, and picking up Stackpole, said, "Stand up on your two feet. I've done up bear pretty well; haven't I, Mrs. Warren." Meantime, Harvey had been busily occupied in pulling apart the branches on the fire, and trying to extinguish it, for it was in danger of spreading, the grass and leaves being quite dry.

All were now obliged to aid in stamping out the flames, as they crinkled along; and the fire would have been a very dangerous one, if it had not been for Harvey's presence of mind and active exertions.

The clock struck one just as the party from the parsonage reached home.

Stackpole had scarcely recovered his wits, and Jack Jimson slunk away to his own room, mortified and provoked, but not penitent.

CHAPTER IX.

REPROOF.

THE next day, when Mr. Warren returned home, Mrs. Warren gave him a laughable account of the doings of the preceding night.

"My dear," said he, "I think in this case prevention would have been better than cure. You might have taken authority upon yourself in my absence, and given those boys a severe lecture."

"But the other boys, the day-scholars, would have done the mischief without Jack and Stackpole," urged the young wife.

"You might have sent Thomas to give Debby warning," suggested the husband, gravely.

"Now don't take it so seriously, Albertus; boys will be boys, and it may be well to overlook the offence."

"Boys will be boys. How frequently that means, sinners will be sinners. No excuse, however, is it for the sins they commit."

"I am sorry to have displeased you," said the little lady, with tears in her eyes.

"Do not make yourself unhappy about the affair, Maria. Yours was an error in judgment, pardonable in one so young and inexperienced; but I trust you will, in future, by a more distant reserve, gain and keep the respect of our pupils. I like to have you lively and bright; but at the same time, you should maintain the dignity of a matron and a clergyman's wife."

"And you will forgive me, and the boys, too, — there's a dear good man," said she, in her most winning way. "They need not know that you have heard a word about it," she continued, with an appealing look that the fond husband could not resist.

"Well, be it so. I must not even reprimand Thomas for the part he took in the farce — say you so, wife?"

"Indeed, you must not; for he acted entirely according to my orders. Clarence had told me a wondrous tale of a bear, related to him by Jack Jimson. On that hint I acted."

Mrs. Warren, whose feelings were as quick and variable as the motions of a wind-tossed leaf, now laughed heartily, as she thought of the appearance and fierce growling of the redoubtable Thomas.

Mr. Warren could not be as severe upon his pretty young wife as he thought her enjoyment of the last night's adventures demanded, and wisely decided that he would keep a stricter watch over the boys than he had done hitherto.

Mrs. Warren had a long talk with the four boys in the library that evening. She assumed a won-

4

derfully dignified manner, and told them she had come to give them a severe lecture, which was to be their punishment. "That is," said she, "the punishment justly merited by Jack and Stackpole."

"It is punishment enough to be associated with such mean fellows as Harvey Amadore and Clanth Wothe," said Jack, impertinently. "I always despised telltales."

"So did I," echoed the toady.

It was somewhat difficult for the young matron to maintain her assumed dignity. She was ready to laugh; but controlling herself, she said, —

"I suppose you are so honorable that you don't like eavesdroppers, either. But I, unfortunately, must confess to the odious character. I happened, accidentally, to overhear your whole plan for the last night's raid; and, therefore, you must not accuse either Harvey or Clarence of being a telltale. I told them much more than they knew about the affair from you. Indeed, you must be very sorry for what has happened, and be more circumspect for the future."

Having thus discharged what she believed to be her duty, Mrs. Warren went to her husband's study to give him an account of her success. He was much amused, but shook his head doubtfully when she boasted of her grave and almost overwhelming dignity of manner.

The guilty boys wondered much from day to day

why they received no reprimand from Mr. Warren.
At length they concluded that Mrs. Warren had
her own private reasons for not informing the master of the affair. Occasionally, on the play-ground,
Jack and Stackpole would be saluted by some of
the other boys with a growl, which made them very
angry. It was evident that every boy in the school
knew all about the adventures of that memorable
evening, for, besides growling, they sometimes gob-
bled like a turkey-cock. Bully Jack *seemed* to have
quite forgotten the dollar Clarence loaned to him
for Debby; but his being a debtor probably ac-
counted for his keeping very shy of Clarence for a
while, and for his desisting from teasing the delicate boy, as he had previously done — a forbearance that was very gratifying to Clarence.

This forbearance, however, was not of long dura-
tion, judging from the following letter from Clarence to Mrs. Rose : —

RACEVILLE, November 10, 18—.

DEAR MAMMA : I, wish I didn't cry so easily.
You know I can't help it. I think that is one reason why the boys tease me so cruelly.

The other night — it was last week — I was in
bed fast asleep, when suddenly a shower of cold
water came upon my face, and startled me out of
bed. My window by some means had been opened
far enough to put in a big syringe. Jack Jimson
and Stackpole Clap were spirting the water over

me; and when I begged them not to do it, they only kept on the more. They stood on a couple of chairs below the window, and could look in upon me, for it was moonlight. I begged them to stop, over and over again, and couldn't help crying; but Jack only said, " Don't waste so much salt water when you have plenty of fresh water."

I said, " I shall tell Mr. Warren of this."

Jack said, " If you do, it will be the worse for you. We'll torment you the more." And Stackpole added, " Yes, we'll worry your very life out if you complain of us."

Then they went off, and I, shivering and shaking, lighted my candle, for I have matches in my room, and got on some dry night-clothes. Then I wrapped myself up in a blanket that wasn't wet, and after a while I got to sleep. The next morning I had a cold in my head, but to-day I feel quite well.

I cry in school sometimes, and then the boys make up hideous faces at me, and draw caricatures of me with what they call my " square mouth." It seems, when I cry, that I open my mouth wide, and in some queer shape.

Don't you think, dear mamma, they are awfully cruel?

I don't know what I should do if Harvey Amadore were not here. He protects me as much as he can; but I am afraid to tell him of a great

many things, for fear they should know it and make
the matter worse.

The day-scholars almost all make fun of me, and
on the play-ground they will not choose me when
they take sides for base-ball or shinney. They say
I am such a gal-boy they don't want me ; and so I
am obliged to stand on one side looking on, and
feeling like a little fool.

I do wish you would let me come home. It
don't seem to me that I can stay here any longer.
I've thought a hundred times that I would run away.

Do ask papa if I may come home. I really don't
care whether I get an education or not. You know,
dear mamma, we are rich enough, and I think I
already know enough for a gentleman ; and I should
like to be a merchant, and make money, as papa has,
and then I am sure nobody would laugh at me.

Now, please, dear mamma, ask papa if I may
come home and go into his counting-room. What
is the use of so much learning unless I meant to be
a minister or a lawyer? Do coax papa to let me
give up my studies. I know you will feel very
sorry for your poor   CLARENCE.

P. S. I wish you would send me a nice parcel
of cake and candies. We have plenty to eat, but
sometimes, when I feel very sad, I should like
something sweet and good, especially when I am in
my own room at night.

CHAPTER X.

MORE MISCHIEF.

CLARENCE stood in need of sympathy, and yet so hard-hearted were the boys, generally, that he received very little. To Harvey, under an injunction of secrecy, he communicated the affair about which he had written to his mother. They were sitting together in Harvey's room, when they had the following chat : —

" Now, Clarence, let me advise you not to allow the boys to see that you mind their teasing. Put on a brave face, and try to have a brave heart, too. Don't let them see you cry, if you can possibly help it. They enjoy calling you cry-baby. I am really attached to you, Clarence, and if it were right I would fight every one of them for insulting you, because I consider you my friend. I have promised Mr. Warren not to get into a quarrel with Jack and Stackpole ; and I know it would be wrong ; but the old Adam is so strong, or, rather, the old Cain, that I am tempted to give them a good drubbing."

" I with you would," said Clarence, doubling up his small fist and grinding his pretty teeth.

Harvey laughingly replied, " *You* would do it if

you could, it seems; but no, Clarence," he continued, "that is not the proper way to resent an
injury; it is contrary to my principles and to my
better feelings. But rely upon me as your friend,
and I promise to do all for you as a friend that lies in
my power, without doing what I know to be wrong."

"But they do fight in English *cools*," urged Clarence.

"It is a barbarous custom," was the reply, "and
they have fags, too, whom they treat unmercifully.
You would fare worse in one of those large English
schools than you do here. Very few boys are as
comfortable at school as we are — there are so few
of us, and Mr. and Mrs. Warren are so very kind."

"I think it a cruel thing anyhow, to thend a boy
away from home," said Clarence, dolorously.

"Why, we have got to mingle with all sorts of
men when we get to be men ourselves, and we
should not be fit for the strife — the rough and
tumble of the world — if we were always coddled
up at home. Come, come, as Longfellow says, —

'In the world's broad field of battle,
 In the bivouac of life,
Be not like dumb, driven cattle —
 Be a hero in the strife.'"

"I never thall be a hero, only one like Mithter
Horner, ' who sat in the corner,' " said Clarence,
merrily.

"And you had rather . pull plums out of a mince-pie, and cry, ' What a big boy am I?' than attend to your studies here, although you may have some rough treatment, and become a strong and a good man. Every man who is truly wise and truly good is, in my opinion, a hero."

Here the bell rang for evening prayers, and the boys hastened to the parlor. Neither Jack nor Stackpole was there, and after waiting some minutes, Mr. Warren commenced reading a chapter in the Bible, and before it was finished the two boys came stealing in, with a guilty look. It was evident they had been in some mischief. And so they had.

For some time past they had been planning how they could break up the intimacy between Harvey and Clarence. They could not, bad and mean as they were — they could not but respect Harvey Amadore. He was an excellent scholar. They knew him to be brave. Not only had he physical courage, and, if he thought it right, could fight like a young savage, but he had moral courage. When he thought himself doing his duty, ridicule had no more effect upon him than it would have upon a bright star. He was as much above it as that same star — a rare thing, especially among boys. Besides, he was generous, — a very popular virtue, — and remarkably good natured, though quick tempered. With the day-scholars he was a universal favorite, and under the broad shelter of his friendship Clarence was protected from many an insult.

Now, Jack and Stackpole determined to break up this friendship. They knew they could not do it by talking against Clarence, or by striving more than ever to render him ridiculous. And so they contrived an infamous plan for the purpose.

They wrote a letter, addressed to Mrs. Rose, in which Harvey was mentioned as a hypocrite.

"He pretends," they wrote, "to be very pious, and Mr. and Mrs. Warren don't see through him; but I, who know him better, I do. He is all outside show. I keep on good terms with him, because it is for my interest. He is a sort of protection to me, because he is so much bigger and stronger than I am; but as for believing in his religion, I say, mamma, I don't believe in it at all; and when I can get a chance I shall shake him off, for I do despise hypocrites, or *hypricots*, as you know I used to write the word.

"I believe, too, Harvey is of very mean origin, not a bit of a gentleman, as I am, for he wears the meanest clothes that ever you saw.

"Now, dear mamma, this is a secret between ourselves. I would not have you let it out for the world, for I must for a while longer keep on good terms with the fellow.

"I am, my dear mamma, your loving

"CLARENCE."

As soon as the boys left the library, after prayers, Stackpole followed Harvey to his room, and told him that he found that letter on the play-ground, and supposed it had been dropped there. It was not directed, nor scaled, and for that reason he and Jack Jimson had read it. Finding it concerned Harvey, they decided it was best to hand it to him.

"Concerns me!" exclaimed Harvey.

"Yes, indeed. I leave you to read it."

As there was no address upon the outside of the letter, Harvey thought it might be intended for him, and read it with absolute amazement. Could it be possible that his friend was so despicably mean and false? The handwriting was Clarence's, as well as the signature. Long did he ponder over that base letter, and hours passed before he could compose himself to sleep.

In the morning Harvey examined the letter more carefully. He at length concluded that he would offer it to Clarence without a word of explanation. He did so immediately after breakfast; and the utter amazement of Clarence, on reading it, was not counterfeited. It was unmistakably perfectly natural.

"Who could have done it? Who could have done it?" he exclaimed, his eyes filling with tears.

Harvey then told him how he had received it, and the story that was told about it.

"O, what a wicked, wicked lie! I will tell

them tho to their faitheth," said Clarence, weeping violently. " They would rob me of my friend."

" No, Clarence, they .will not. I will accuse them of this forgery, for forgery it really is. It will be better for you to keep quiet about it."

" How can I! How can I!" sobbed the heart-wounded boy.

There was always an hour for recreation before school on the play-ground.

Harvey took the two villanous boys aside, and said, in an assured and angry tone, —

" What could have tempted you to write this abominable letter?"

" I write it! How dare you accuse me?" exclaimed Jack.

" Or me either?" added Stackpole, in a tremulous voice.

" Now, boys, if you don't confess it at once, I will carry the letter directly to Mr. Warren, and he will settle the matter with you. It is a forgery, and the probability is, he will expel you from school."

Stackpole's crimson face and trembling limbs betrayed his guilt, while Jack's brazen countenance assumed an air of defiance.

Harvey turned from them, and took a few steps towards the house, while a whispered consultation was going on between the two partners in wickedness.

" Stop a minute. Let me see the letter," cried Jack.

Harvey said, calmly, "Not till you acknowledge that you wrote it."

"Then I'll take it from you. Hold him, Stackpole." But Stackpole held off.

"Coward!" exclaimed Jack, looking at his compeer with extreme disgust and contempt.

Harvey stood unmoved, his eye fixed upon Jack boldly and resolutely. Jack knew his strength and his courage, and did not attempt to take the letter from him by force.

"You acknowledge the forgery in action if not in words; why else should you be so anxious to take it from me? Besides, you have not yet learned from me its contents. How guilt betrays itself! Look at Stackpole as he stands there, the very image of guilt itself."

"I didn't write it; he did," blurted out Stackpole.

"Mean, despicable fool!" exclaimed Jack.

"Now, boys, perhaps I ought to expose you to Mr. Warren; but I am sorry for you — so young and so wicked. What will you come to? I beg of you to reflect upon your conduct, and to repent of it. I forgive you, and so will Clarence; but you must ask forgiveness of God."

So saying, Harvey took the letter from his pocket, tore it to atoms, and scattered it to the wind.

The two boys slunk away to a corner of the play-ground, abashed before the courage and manliness of their honest school-fellow.

CHAPTER XI.

A SUDDEN CHANGE.

EARLY in December the boys were having their first snow-balling on the play-ground.

Though wrapped up warmly, and wearing kid gloves, Clarence shivered, and complained bitterly of the cold. His delicate frame had not been inured to hardship of any kind.

The play-ground was on one side of the parsonage. A large gate opened upon the main road, and from the gate a carriage-way led to the house through the grounds. A market-cart with a scraggy, miserable screw of a horse, driven by a woman, entered the gate, and passing through the play-ground, stopped in front of the house.

" There's crow's-meat," exclaimed Jack Jimson.

" You mean the horth ; but what doth the woman driving the rack o' boneth look like?" said Clarence, laughing immoderately.

" Very like a scare-crow," was the saucy reply.

The boys had now gathered in a cluster near the cart, looking on with curious eyes to see what the woman wanted.

" Poor creature. She muth have come to beg, for there ith nothing in the cart," said Clarence.

" She lookth more like a beggar than anything elth," added Clarence.

" She looks like a respectable woman, as she is," whispered Harvey. " Do be careful not to make such impertinent remarks ; she will hear you ;" then stepping quickly to the side of the cart, he assisted the woman to alight.

" Thank you, sir," said she ; then looking round upon the group of boys, she added, " I've come for my son, who is here at school with Mr. Warren."

" Your son? He is not here. There are only four of us at the parsonage," said Harvey, as he fastened the poor horse to a post.

Meantime, the other three had gathered to the spot.

The boys were laughing at Harvey's politeness to the meanly-dressed woman. She surveyed them attentively, and at length exclaimed, —

" Can that be him?" pointing to Jack Jimson. " I wonder if he will own his mother."

" The woman must be beside herself," thought Harvey, as she advanced towards Jack, and holding out her hand, said, " Are you my son?"

" A good joke! A capital joke! Your son, indeed!" replied Jack, with a horse-laugh, echoed by Stackpole.

" My son is called Clarence Rose," said she, in a faltering voice.

At this they set up a shout ; and Jack, seizing Clarence by the waist, with both hands held him

" You are my son, then ! " Page 63.

high in the air, saying, ". This dolly-boy is Clanth Wothe."

" Set me down," shrieked Clarence. " Set me down, I thay ! "

Jack placed the shivering boy on his feet, by the side of the woman, who looked at him with evident disappointment, as she said, —

" You are my son, then. You are a pretty little boy, but so very little? Kiss your mother."

Clarence drew back frightened, and whispered to Harvey, " The woman mutht be crazy."

" I must see Mr. Warren, the master, right off," said she.

" Come into the house; you have staid too long in the cold already," said · Harvey, kindly, leading the way, and showing the stranger into the parlor, while the others stood without, wondering much at this mysterious affair.

" Did you ever see this woman before, Clarence ? " asked Stackpole.

" Never in my life," was the reply.

" The equipage don't quite suit the style of the elegant New Yorker, with his fiery-fine trappings," said Jack.

At this moment Mr. Warren opened the door, and called Clarence to come in. He held a letter in his hand, and looked very soberly as he gave another letter to Clarence.

" I ought to have received these letters two or

three days since," said Mr. Warren. "They have been unaccountably delayed. Take yours to the library and read it by yourself, and then come to me in the parlor."

Sure enough, the letter was addressed to Master Clarence Rose, and read as follows : —

My Dear Boy : You have hitherto considered yourself my son, and it was not my intention to have undeceived you till you came of age. But misfortunes have come upon me like an armed host. I am a bankrupt, not worth a dollar in the world, and I must now give you up to your own mother. She will come to take you to her own home a few days after this reaches you.

My wife adopted you when you were not quite three years old, and has been, I fear, only too tender a mother to you. She has wept many hours at the loss of property we have sustained, but more at the necessity for giving up her petted Clarence, -all unfitted, as he is, for the roughness of his future life. I know you will feel the change keenly, but I trust you will be a good, obedient son to your poor but honest mother. Your "mamma" sends tenderest love and heartfelt wishes for your happiness; she will write to you herself, when her feelings allow. I shall never cease to take a deep interest in your welfare, my dear Clarence.

Faithfully yours,

Samuel Rose.

After reading this astounding letter, Clarence was like one who had received a stunning blow physically. He seemed not able to speak or to move.

Mr. Warren came to him at length, and aroused him from this stupor by telling him that he must make immediate preparations to leave with his mother, Mrs. Paverley. She was now taking some refreshment in the dining-room, and must start within an hour from that time. Mr. Warren was much moved at the sight of the wild distress of Clarence.

"My poor boy," said he, "it will be a great change for you; but God has ordered it, and it may prove the best thing that could have befallen you. It depends on yourself whether you make the best use of what now seems to you adversity."

Clarence threw himself upon a sofa, hid his face, and sobbed like an infant.

"Mr. Rose has written to me," continued Mr. Warren. "He has explained to me that your mother was left a widow, with six children, without the means of support, and, not without reluctance on her part, gave you to Mrs. Rose, on condition that you should be given back to your own mother, if the circumstances of your adopted parents should change for the worse. Mr. and Mrs. Rose are going to California, where he hopes to find some employment. You have now a motive to exertion, Clarence, and you must cheer up and go quietly with your mother."

5

Poor Clarence continued to weep without uttering a word.

" Come, my boy, there is no help for this misfortune, as you consider it. Summon up resolution, and go with me to pack up your trunks."

Mr. Warren led the weeping boy to his room, and soon his luggage was ready to be placed in the cart.

Clarence begged Mr. Warren to let him go without taking leave of his schoolmates, to which the master consented, but led him to the dining-room to see Mrs. Warren, who had petted and indulged the pretty boy almost as much as had Mrs. Rose.

While Mrs. Paverley was enjoying a lunch, the kind young wife filled a basket with sandwiches and doughnuts for refreshments on the road; and when she handed it to Clarence she wept so vehemently that she could scarcely say " good by." He could only sob out the word " kind — kind."

" Poor little lad, he looks sickly," said his mother.

" He is only delicate, a hot-house plant, that will require care and consideration. I need not tell his own mother to treat him tenderly," said Mr. Warren.

" I don't know what I *shall* do with him. He just seems fit to be wrapped up in wool, like a young chicken taken from the old hen," said the mother, dolefully:

" He shall be wrapped in wool to-day," said Mr.

Warren, smiling; "for here is a thick, warm blanket, my good wife has provided for him."

The big trunks almost filled the market-cart. There was scarcely room for the board in front on which Mrs. Paverley and Clarence were seated. Mr. Warren was obliged to lift the weeping boy into the cart, and to put the blanket around him, as he bade him a tender farewell.

The miserable horse had been well fed, and Mrs. Paverley, taking the reins in her hand, started him off on a full trot.

"We've got twenty mile to ride, and Patchy must do his best, or we shan't be home to-night," said she. "But don't cry so, my son. The gentleman says you were baptized Clarence Rose, and I must call you so, though your real name was Azariah Paverley. It was hard times with me, or I should not have parted with you. I had six then. God has taken three of them to himself, and now I have only Lucy, Peter, and you. I hope you won't despise us because we are poor. You know it is our heavenly Father who chooses our lot for us, and he does all things well."

Clarence had not yet spoken a word, though they had now passed over half a dozen miles.

"I am afraid you are cold," continued Mrs. Paverley, drawing her thin shawl more closely around her. "Say, my son, are you comfortable?"

"Yith."

" What did you say?"

" I thaid yith."

Mrs. Paverley exclaimed, " Now I know it's my own Azariah ; that was just his own way of speaking when he was that pretty white-headed boy. Why, you are old enough to speak plain. You used to say, ' I faid of Wob.' That was your oldest brother, who used to tease you. Don't you remember him?"

" I do not remember Rob," said Clarence, quite glibly.

After travelling about twelve miles, the rack of bones called Patchy could not be induced to move faster than a walk, and finally refused to stir another step.

The air grew chill ; a sudden snow flurry almost blinded the eyes of the travellers, and night was coming on rapidly. They were more than a mile from any dwelling-house.

" What are we to do·now?" asked Clarence, mournfully.

" We must let Patchy rest a while," she replied, with her teeth chattering and her face blue with cold.

" You are very cold, marm ; will you have my blanket wrapped around you?" said Clarence.

" Thank you, thank you ; I'll share it with you," said she, delighted with this first act of thoughtfulness from her son.

Patchy was guided to a spot protected by a large

pine tree ; and soon after the comfortable arrangement with the blanket had been made, Clarence fell
asleep, with his head resting on his mother's
shoulder.

After having remained a full hour under the tree,
the snow flurry passed away, and the moon peered
out between the driving clouds.

Without awakening Clarence, Mrs. Paverley succeeded in starting Patchy on the road. Apparently
the poor beast bethought himself that he was on the
way home, for he made his lean shanks move
swiftly over the snow-covered ground ; and when
Clarence awoke, it was at the door of his mother's
cottage.

CHAPTER XII.

THE BROWN COTTAGE.

" WHERE am I?" cried Clarence, awaking from a
sound sleep.

" Home," was the reply.

A faint light shone through the small window of
a brown cottage.

" Home! Can it be *my* home?" exclaimed the
poor boy.

The door of the cottage opened, and a young girl
appeared with a flaring candle in her hand.

"Mother, is it you?" said a sweet voice. "I have been so anxious about you! Is my brother with you?"

"Yes, here he is, not more than half awake."

The poor fellow did not move after his mother had alighted from the cart. There he sat, as still as a snow statue.

Mrs. Paverley lifted him in her strong arms, and carried him into the room which was kitchen, dining-room, and parlor. She placed him on a wooden bench, near a small cooking-stove, in which a fire was still burning.

Clarence had never been in the dwelling of a poor person since he left his home ten years before.

"Where is Peter?" asked the mother.

"Gone to bed, long ago," said Lucy.

"Rouse him up. Patchy must be fed and cared for."

Clarence sat by the stove, every bone and every muscle aching with the jolting he had undergone.

"You shall have some hot sage tea," said his mother.

"I see Lucy has kept water hot, and potatoes, too," added Mrs. Paverley, looking into the stove oven.

Lucy, having called Pete, returned, and went to work to have supper ready for the travellers. She drew a large pine table near the stove, and spread a brown cloth upon it. While thus employed she said to Clarence, —

" You must be very tired and hungry. You had a tedious journey."

There was something wonderfully soothing in this sweet voice, and Clarence looked inquiringly at the face of his sister. It was a lovely face, expressive of uncommon sweetness of disposition, and at the same time decidedly intellectual.

Peter came bounding down the narrow staircase, from the attic, and seizing the hand of Clarence with his own rough and brown one, shouted, —

" How are you, fellow? Yellow kid gloves. Now if that ain't jolly ! "

" Pete, go instantly and take care of Patchy," said the mother.

Patchy had already found his way to the barn. Peter took good care of him, but left the trunks in the cart.

The contents of Mrs. Warren's basket, with the addition of hot potatoes, made an excellent meal, which Clarence did not reject ; neither did he refuse the sage tea, unpalatable as it was to his fastidious taste. Peter was not averse to sharing the good things, when he came in from the barn.

After the refreshing supper was finished, Mrs. Paverley said, cheerfully, to Lucy, " Come, my child, take the Bible and read a few verses."

With that sweet, melodious voice, which seemed the most suitable music for the Psalms of David, Lucy read the following verses : —

" Bow down thine ear, O Lord ; hear me, for I am poor and needy.

" Preserve my soul ; for I am holy. O thou my God, save thy servant that trusteth in thee.

" Be merciful unto me, O Lord ; for I cry unto thee daily.

" Rejoice the soul of thy servant ; for unto thee, O Lord, do I lift up my soul.

" For thou, Lord, art good, and ready to forgive, and plenteous in mercy unto all them that call upon thee.

" Give ear, O Lord, unto my prayer, and attend to the voice of my supplications."

The mother and daughter knelt, and Clarence followed their example. The mother uttered a fervent thanksgiving for a safe journey, and for the blessing of having her son restored to her, and ended with the Lord's Prayer.

Clarence was then shown into a very small, but clean room, adjoining the kitchen. In spite of his fatigue and sorrow, he soon fell asleep, and slept as soundly on the straw bed as if it had been his usual spring-mattress.

It was just nine o'clock, the next morning, when the mother stepped quietly to the bedside of the sleeping Clarence. His soft, light hair fell in disorder about a face flushed with an almost infantile rosy hue. One small, delicate hand lay upon the rough coverlet, which contrasted strangely with the fine linen wristband and gold sleeve-buttons. In the other hand was an embroidered handkerchief, which had been saturated with tears from the eyes of the pretty sleeper.

Mrs. Paverley gazed at her son with a mingled feeling of pity and admiration. Through the open door she beckoned to Lucy, who immediately stepped to her side.

" Beautiful," whispered Lucy. She now remembered when her little playmate was taken from her, and the tears that it cost her. The tears that now moistened her large gray eyes were tears of joy.

Suddenly Clarence awoke, and looked directly into those loving eyes. He drew his face beneath the covering, exclaiming, " Where am I ? "

" At your own home, my brother," was the gentle reply.

" Yes, my son ; and you must get up and have your breakfast," said another, not as gently, but with real kindness, as she closed the door.

After a few moments, Clarence gave a little tap on the door, and said, —

" Pleath, marm, I don't obtherve any wath bathin and ewer."

" Peter always washes himself at the pump," said Mrs. Paverley ; " but for this once you shall have a wash basin in your room."·

A tin basin and a coarse towel were handed in.

To Clarence, who had been accustomed to all the

means and appliances of "modern improvement,"
this rough way of making his morning ablutions
was a severe trial. He seemed, figuratively, to
have jumped from a hot bath into a snow-drift.

Was it the rough towel, that almost took the skin
off his face, that brought tears to his eyes?

After a while he partly opened the door, and said,
" I thould like my drething-cathe."

" Come to breakfast, my son ; you cannot have it
now."

The breakfast consisted of mush and milk, and
some of the remaining doughnuts.

The poor boy had no appetite for his solitary
breakfast.

At one end of the kitchen was a wooden bench,
on which stood two large wash-tubs. At one of
these tubs was Lucy, employed in washing. She
had been thus occupied for more than two hours
that morning before Clarence was awake.

The mother had left the other tub to attend to
Clarence.

From an old black teapot Mrs. Paverley poured
a cup of sage tea into a bowl, and sweetened it with
molasses.

" You must take this herb tea, boy. It will do
you good. Don't you feel stiff after your long
ride ? "

" I do. Every bone in my body acheth."

" Then take this good hot tea," urged the mother.

" I can't, I can't, I can't ! " exclaimed Clarence ; and unable longer to control himself, he burst into a violent fit of crying and sobbing.

" I am sorry for you ; but you must not be such a baby. It's a thousand pities that you should have been spoiled. Why, your brother Peter, though a year younger than you, is a mighty deal more of a man."

In spite of his mother's remonstrance, the poor boy dropped his head upon the table and continued to weep vehemently.

The tears of the sympathetic sister fell too fast to count them ; but she refrained from offering a consolatory word, having been told by her mother not to treat the boy too tenderly.

The sound of wheels was now heard, and soon after Peter rushed in, saying, at the top of his voice, —

" Them trunks are lost ; no finding 'em no-where."

" My trunths lost ! " exclaimed Clarence, raising his head from the table, and regarding Peter with amazement.

" Yes, sir-ee ! When I went to the barn this morning early, I looked into the cart where they were left, and not a sign of a trunk was there. Then I came in and told mother. Without giving me a morsel of breakfast, she made me start off to the village to inquire after them. Nothing has been heard of 'em there. Mother, I'm hungry as a wolf," continued Peter, gazing wishfully at the doughnuts.

"I've kept some potatoes hot in the ashes for you," said the mother, poking among the embers.

Clarence shoved the doughnuts to the other side of the table where Peter had seated himself.

"Help yourthelf, if you pleathe," said he.

A smile passed over the rough features of the stout younger brother, — whether caused by the childish lisp of his pretty brother, or induced by the kindly offer, it would be difficult to say. At all events, the doughnuts rapidly disappeared, and the potatoes followed in quick succession. The rejected sage tea was swallowed without taking the bowl from Peter's mouth, till he came to the last drop.

All at once he seemed to recollect himself, as Clarence said, in a doleful voice, —

"My clothe and every thing gone! What can I do?"

"O, here's a letter for you, from the post-office, Master Clarence Rose; and a box is in the entry with the same name on it. I'll bring it in. I found it at the hotel. It came in the stage."

So saying, Peter lugged in the box, strong fellow that he was, and told Clarence to take it up and carry it to his room.

Clarence tried in vain to lift the box, for though it was not large, it was heavy.

" What a baby you are ! " exclaimed Pete, lifting the box and striding across the kitchen proudly.

When he had deposited it in the small bedroom, he called out, " Sugar plums for baby, I guess. Come, let's see. Hammer and tongs ! Let's open her."

Pete knocked away with a will, and soon the contents of the box were displayed.

Clarence seized a letter lying on the top, and finding it was from his " mamma," read it eagerly, while Pete hauled out the other contents and heaped them upon the floor.

Every thing that had belonged to Clarence, even from childhood, had been gathered by Mrs. Rose and forwarded to her darling. Even many of his playthings — balls, tops, battledoors, skates, &c.

Clarence was aroused from the perusal of the kind letter by the loud laughter of Pete, and his exclamation, —

" Jimminy, what a thing ! You would look like a fire-hang-bird, with this on your back ! "

Pete was holding up a *brand* new paletot, of fine blue broadcloth, lined with scarlet flannel.

Mrs. Rose mentioned in her letter that this garment had been made and paid for before the failure of Mr. Rose.

There were numerous gay cravats that had been thrown aside, and other articles of wearing apparel that had been outgrown. But what Clarence saw

with the greatest pleasure was a number of books,
— in short, his whole miscellaneous library, from
Mother Goose and Cock Robin to Prescott's "Conquest of Mexico."

Pete poked his arms into the sleeves of the paletot, and turning out as much of the scarlet lining as
possible, went capering into the kitchen, crying, —
" Ain't I fine ! jolly fine ! "

The associations connected with the childhood of
Clarence, and the letter, quite overcame the boy,
and he threw himself upon the bed and cried aloud.

" Boo-hoo ! Boo-hoo ! " exclaimed Pete ; " a thir-
teen-year-old baby ! "

" Be quiet, Pete ; take off that overcoat, and go
about your business.   You shan't tease Clarence,"
said the mother.

" The boys will throw mud at him if he wears
this thing," replied Pete, throwing the paletot on the
floor, and giving it a contemptuous kick.

Pete was a fair specimen of a " muscular " boy.
He had swung his hands, not in play-gymnastics,
but with axe in hand, since he was nine years old.
Hoe, rake, and spade were his other implements
for exercise ; and his broad shoulders and sturdy
arms, his tough, hard hands, and his big feet,
matched well with his wide, expanded chest, and
his thick neck.   He thought himself manly because
he was physically strong.   But that was a great
mistake.   He was strong like a beast of burden.

That kind of strength has its use ; but it is not the highest kind of strength.   Something more is wanting for a man, " the lord of creation."

CHAPTER XIII.

A PLEASANT MEETING.

WHEN Clarence had been in his new home a few weeks, he would scarcely have been recognized by his schoolmates at the parsonage.

The gay paletot had been exchanged at a tailor's in the neighboring village for a suit of coarse gray cloth and some other needed garments.   Thick " cowhide " boots and a woollen cap completed his attire.

One evening, at supper time, Pete did not appear at the usual hour.   He generally was quite anxious for supper.   It was a cruelly cold winter evening, and, as hour after hour passed, Mrs. Paverley and Lucy became seriously alarmed.

At length, about ten o'clock, something seemed to be thrown against the front door.   Lucy ran to open it.

There was Pete, in a dreadful condition.   Somebody had helped him home, for he had been quite unable to walk.

He had been trying his strength with a boy nearly twice his own age and size, and had been furiously beaten. One of his eyes was so swollen that it was entirely closed, and his face was covered with blood. In short, he was bruised from head to foot, and his boasted strength was so far gone, that his mother and sister were obliged to use theirs to lift the boy into the house.

"Where have you been? and what have you been about?" exclaimed the mother, as they laid Pete upon a "settle" * before the fire.

Pete was so completely chilled that he could not answer. Indeed, from the injuries he had received, and the severe cold, he was almost insensible.

Clarence ran for a sponge, — which was among the articles sent in the box, — and with some luke-warm water washed the blood from Pete's face, while Mrs. Paverley drew off his boots, and rubbed the almost frozen feet. Lucy put on the tea-kettle, to make some of her mother's sovereign remedy for all complaints — sage tea.

After using these simple restoratives till Pete seemed to be thawed out, the mother again questioned him.

When he attempted to answer, they found that he lisped quite as much as Clarence; for in his fierce fight he had bitten his own tongue.

---

* Settle. A wooden seat for four persons, with a high back to keep off the cold air.

" I tan't tell you," he uttered with great difficulty, with his mouth open and his swollen tongue protruding from his mouth.

Lucy was agreeably surprised to find her brother Clarence so tender and helpful. He seemed to have forgotten all the rough usage and unkindness he had received from Pete, and he showed unusual thoughtfulness in the means he used to alleviate the sufferings of the young bully, who, in trying his strength, had nearly lost his life.

In consequence of Pete's inability to go about his usual work, Clarence was obliged to take his place. Patchy came under his special care, besides two pigs that were to be fed, wood to be brought in, and kindling to be chopped.

The day but one after Pete's *frolic*, Clarence had to drive into the neighboring village, — we might as well call it Hodgeton, though that was not really its name. Well, Clarence was obliged to tackle that rack of bones, Patchy, to the cart, and drive into Hodgeton with the week's washing. From the hotel in the village, Mrs. Paverley was regularly supplied with a quantity of clothing, and her principal source of revenue was the wash-tub.

Like the famous Giles Jolt, who, when he was sleeping on the road, and some rogues stole his horse, and when he awoke found himself alone in the cart, exclaimed, " Am I Giles Jolt, or am I not? If so, I've lost a horse; if not, I've found a

6

cart," Clarence might have doubted his own iden-
tity, so strange it was for him to be driving that
forlorn beast in that miserable cart.

And yet, there was a new sense of power, as he
held the reins, that was not disagreeable. He was
somebody who had the control of another body, and
he drove up to the door of the cottage for the baskets quite valiantly. Yet when he stood by the
fire, warming his hands, tears were in his eyes.

Lucy took the small hands in her own, and chafed
them, saying, " I will go to the village for you,
brother ; it is too hard for you."

" No, no," he replied, " I am not crying. I with
to go mythelf. I'm only cold."

" That's right," said the mother, as she brought
a warm blanket to wrap about the delicate boy.

" And here is the muffler for your ears that I
finished last night," said Lucy, tying the woollen
comforter about the neck and head of her brother ;
and then she helped him in putting the baskets in
the cart.

Thus defended from the cold, Clarence drove
Patchy quite cheerily to the village, and stopped
before the hotel. As he was taking one of the
large baskets out of the cart, a pleasant, familiar
voice greeted his ear.

" How are you, Clarence ! Let me help you
with the baskets. It's a bitter day for you to be
out."

" Harvey Amadore! How came you here?" was the surprised exclamation that followed.

" I am here for the winter vacation. Let's hand in the baskets, and put Patchy under cover ; then we will go in and have a good talk."

So saying, Harvey seized one of the baskets and carried it into the hotel, while Clarence with much difficulty dragged another along.

" Come, Sam Patch," said Harvey, gayly, as he drove the miserable steed into the stable, while Clarence looked after his friend — to him, indeed, a friend in need.

Soon the two boys were cosily seated by a rousing fire in the " inn's best room." A table, with arrangements for two persons, was soon spread, and a smoking-hot dinner, of broiled chickens and stewed oysters, was placed upon the table.

Poor Clarence looked at the savory meal with longing eyes.

" Come, Clarence, let us draw up and take our dinner before it is cold," said Harvey.

Clarence hesitated, and colored deeply. He had no money. His pride revolted at being obliged to make the confession ; besides, he had always thought Harvey to be in very moderate circumstances.

Harvey placed a chair by the table for Clarence, saying, —

" I ordered dinner for two. I am sure you will

not refuse to keep a friend company, who would otherwise have had a solitary meal. "

" But, but," began Clarence. Harvey interrupted him.

" None of your *buts*, or *ifs*, or *ands*, old fellow. This, for the time being, is my home, and you are my guest."

Thus urged, Clarence took the offered chair, and Harvey seated himself opposite his " guest."

" Shall I say grace?" inquired Harvey, with just the slightest embarrassment.

Clarence nodded assent.

Never before was a meal so welcome to the petted boy, accustomed as he had been in other days to a luxurious table.

" I haven't told you anything about our school," said Harvey, who was enjoying the relishing dinner more in seeing the keen appetite of his friend thus gratified, than by partaking of it himself, though he did set the example by eating heartily, but not immoderately.

" I must tell you about the boys."

" Do, do. I want to hear about them," said Clarence.

" Bully Jimson fought with Daring Dick of the village, and had one eye knocked out."

" That might have happened to my brother Peter, for he wath dreadfully hurt in a fight. Why do boyth fight?"

" Because they are too much afraid of being called cowards; and, besides, they think it is manly. Mr. Warren sent immediately for Jimson's parents, and they carried the poor fellow home."

" What has become of Stackpole Clap?"

" O, to be sure; we have two new boys, whom he toadies just as he toadied Jimson. It is a meanness of nature so deeply rooted, I fear he will never be able to eradicate it. He tried it with me, after you left; but I was so disgusted with it, that I told him, not very politely, that I had a natural aversion to toads and snakes. Since then he has revenged himself by calling me " old graypatch," which nickname the new boys have adopted; but that does not trouble me at all. Mrs. Warren has been, you know, more quiet and dignified since the turkey affair, and Mr. Warren is as good and faithful as ever. I consider him one of the best friends I have had since I have been an orphan. I was sorry to part with you from school, Clarence."

" How did you happen to know my mother " — eagerly inquired Clarence; and in a lower tone he added — " to be a rethpectable woman?"

" I had often seen her in the village and at church, and your sister Lucy was a scholar in the Sunday school when I was a small boy in the same school. She was the very best scholar in her class."

" Then you live near here?" said Clarence.

" Yes. I live just over there, on Linden Hill,"

replied Harvey, pointing to a large stone building, looking almost like a castle.

" The Lindens! That your home!" exclaimed his companion, with wide-open eyes.

" That is my home, a desolate home, for I have neither father nor mother, brother nor sister."

" And ith it all your own?"

" It is; but gladly would I have had dear ones to enjoy it with me. I am going to have a Christmas party. I shall ask the teachers and scholars of the Sunday school, of which I have spoken, to come to the Lindens on Christmas eve; and I want you and your sister to join us there."

Clarence was meditating upon the plain gray dress which Harvey had always worn at Mr. Warren's, and in which he now appeared, and from which he inferred that he was very far from rich, his idea of wealth being very closely associated with fine clothing.

" You do not accept my invitation," said Harvey.

" I haven't any thing fit to wear to a party," said Clarence, doubtfully and dolefully.

" Nonsense. I can't accept such an apology. I shall ask your sister myself. Will you take me home with you now?'

" But will you ride in a cart, with that mitherable apology for a horth?"

" I will go home with you, if you will allow me the pleasure," kindly replied Harvey. " Fetch up

Patchy to the door, if you please, and I will be ready to jump in."

While Clarence went for his humble equipage, Harvey paid the hotel bill, and warmed the blanket which had been brought in from the cart. Harvey sprang into the vehicle at a bound, saying, —

" Let me wrap the blanket around you, and give me the reins ; my hands are tongh, and yours are tender."

Clarence gladly yielded the reins ; and Patchy, stimulated by a plentiful dinner of oats, went off at a brisk pace.

Much wondering, and quite anxious at the prolonged absence of Clarence, Lucy was eagerly looking out of the small front window of the cottage, when Patchy came trotting up to the door. Oats had more to do with his speed than the driver's skill, though Harvey was accountable for both.

Clarence introduced " Mr. Amadore " with evident embarrassment, while Lucy received the visitor calmly, and placed a chair for him without the slightest awkwardness. Mrs. Paverley was in a flutter, wondering what had happened.

Harvey took the offered chair, near the stove, and soon made known the object of his visit,

Lucy said she would be pleased to meet her former teachers and schoolmates of the Sunday school, and she would be glad to have Clarence with her.

Harvey then inquired after Peter, and asked to have him come to the Christmas party,

· "O, dear me," replied Mrs. Paverley, "Pete won't be out of the house for at least two weeks; he's had such a dreadful drubbing. I hope it will be a lesson to him not to go about fighting like a bull-dog."

Harvey soon after hastened homeward, full of kind and benevolent plans for others besides himself. Gifted with a large fortune, his earnest desire was, to make the best possible use of it in doing good.

CHAPTER XIV.

HARDSHIPS.

Now that Peter was disabled, Clarence had to perform all the out-door work at the cottage. He had never before handled an axe. Now he had to cut and split all the wood for the stove, and his hands were blistered with the hard work. He had, besides to feed the horse and a pig. This latter duty was specially disagreeable to the delicate boy.

One evening, rather late, he went to give piggy his supper. It was so dim at the pig-pen that he could not see the place where the contents of the bucket were to be poured into the trough. Piggy became very impatient for his supper, and made it known by loud squeals. Clarence began to be quite frightened; but when the enraged pig jumped upon

the side of the pen, the terrified boy put down the
bucket, and ran into the house, crying out that "the
pig had gone mad, and was going to attack him fu-
riouthly."

Lucy lighted a candle, put it in an old lantern,
and went immediately to see if she could quell the
furious animal; while Mrs. Paverley gave Clarence
a severe scolding for what she called his "silly
fears of a fat pig."

Indeed, in the midst of all the trials incident to
his new situation, his sister Lucy's gentle kindness
was a great alleviation. Lucy Paverley might have
been the original of Wordsworth's sweet poem, entitled "Lucy,"—

> "A maid whom there were none to praise,
>   And very few to love.
> A violet by a mossy stone,
>   Half hidden from the eye!
> Fair as a star, when only one
>   Is shining in the sky."

Mrs. Paverley had frequently remarked that Lucy
took after her father, adding that "he had a mighty
taste for learning, and took to *poetry* as a duck
takes to water."

Although Lucy had had the advantage of only
three winters' schooling, at the common school of
the district, she was a proficient in the three R's,—
"'readin', 'ritin', and 'rithmetic,'"—and had a decided taste for study.

Mr. Paverley had been an invalid for several years before his death, and had been supported by his hard-working wife, with the assistance of Mr. Amadore, the father of Harvey, who was then living at the Lindens. Paverley, when in health, was head gardener at the Lindens, and was really a man of uncommon taste for reading, for one in his position.

It was very true that Lucy more resembled her father in character than she did her less refined mother. She had, too, more genuine sensibility and sentiment than her brother Clarence, in spite of his very different education. That, indeed, had been a hot-house culture, quite unfitting him for the rude encounter of wintry blasts.

For some days after Clarence had undertaken the tasks which had devolved upon Peter, he was so fatigued by these extraordinary labors, that he was obliged to go to bed immediately after supper.

His bedroom now showed a very different appearance from the shabby one that presented itself to the astonished boy on his first arrival.

In the box sent by Mrs. Rose were a number of pretty engravings, some in frames and others without. All of these Lucy had arranged about the small bedroom, and they nearly covered the dingy walls. A neat patchwork bed-quilt covered his bed, and he had even a toilet-table, made, to be sure, of rough boards, but covered with white muslin, an ingenious transformation from Mrs. Paverley's wedding dress. On the toilet-table stood the beautiful dressing-case which came in the box, and had been a Christmas gift to Clarence only a year previously. A few shelves over the toilet-table contained his library.

Mrs. Paverley did not altogether approve of this ministration to the luxurious taste of the effeminate boy, and yet she allowed Lucy to have her own way about the bedroom, with one exception. When Lucy proposed to have a wash-stand purchased in the village, Mrs. Paverley replied, —

" No, no," very decidedly. " He shall go to the well, and wash himself in the tin basin, as Pete does. You *cosset* him too much."

Small as this trial might have been to a resolute boy, who might one day be subjected to the hardships of a soldier's life, it was a severe one to Clarence. He felt as though he would rather " kick the bucket," in a literal sense, than to draw it up from the well; and he frequently salted the water, with which he washed his face and hands, with those " briny drops " which boys usually are ashamed to shed.

And when the thermometer was 10° below zero, as it was the day before Christmas, there was danger of the water's freezing before he could finish his morning ablutions. No wonder that a real " boo-hoo, boo-hoo," accompanied the splash upon his face, and continued when the water froze to the

towel which hung on a roller behind the kitchen
door.

Lucy chafed the aching fingers and warmed them
on her own cheeks, with the comforting assurance
that those fingers were "red, and not white," as
they would have been if they were frozen.

Small comfort in this assurance while the pain
lasted, but great comfort in his sister's warmth and
kindness.

CHAPTER XV.

MERRY CHRISTMAS.

HARVEY AMADORE had been left an orphan at the
age of thirteen, and was now sixteen.

The will of his father was a remarkable one.
By it Harvey was to receive two thousand dollars a
year till he became of age, "to use in his education
and in other ways." He was to have the spending
of this money, as expressed in the will, " that Harvey may learn to use money with *economy* and *gen-
erosity* — to do good to himself and others with
wealth which has been accumulated without a con-
scientious regard to the wants of the poor and
needy. He is, moreover, to make himself and
others as innocently happy as possible with the
liberal allowance granted him during his minority.

Furthermore, he must remember that the estate of which he will in time become possessor, is not the result of his own labor, but was acquired through the labor, care, and painstaking of another; and that he, Harvey Amadore, will be accountable to God for the right use of it. During his minority he must keep a strict account of his expenditures, and render this account quarterly to my executor, Mr. Hosea Fenton, of the city of New York."

The Lindens was Harvey's home when he was not at school, and the spacious mansion was kept in order by the housekeeper. She was a poor relation, a second cousin to Mr. Amadore, and was named by him, in that singular will, as housekeeper at the Lindens during Harvey's minority, with a liberal allowance for herself and for the expense of keeping the place in order.

And now Christmas had come, and was to be merrily kept by the teachers and scholars at the Hodgeton Sunday school.

A tall Christmas tree, a beautiful Norway spruce, was placed in the centre of the circular saloon, at the Lindens. An entrance hall led to this saloon, which occupied a large space in the middle of the house, and was lighted from the beautifully painted window on the roof.

The tree had been firmly fixed in a large block of wood, which was completely covered with running pine and other evergreen vines from the woods.

" Come, Aunty Dotty, come and see my Christmas tree," said Harvey, delighted with its appearance, as it stood with its aspiring top pointing to the
sky, or, rather, the sky-light. He then left the
saloon.

Miss Dorothy Trig was a tall maiden, whom fifty
years had visited somewhat roughly, judging by
the screwed-up mouth which approached her nose
with a pugnacious expression, and the defiant look
of her light gray eyes.

Aunty Dotty, as Harvey called this far-off cousin,
gave her mouth a tighter screw than usual as she
surveyed the tree, and then she gave forth her opinion of it.

" A Christmas tree ! · What heathenish nonsense !
In my childhood it would have been considered the
same sort of thing as a mince-pie was among the
Puritans — a remnant of Popery. But times are
altered," added Aunty Dotty, with a deep sigh, as
she placed her thin arms akimbo, and rolled up
her gray eyes with a woful expression, " times
are altered dreadfully for the worse. I wonder if they mean to transmogrify our country
into a Babylon. I shouldn't wonder if this tree
was a kind of foreshadowing of such an idol as
Nebuchadnezzar set up, or, leastwise, of them they
set up now in Rome."

After this soliloquy, Aunty Dotty turned her
back upon the foreshadowing idol; and retired to
nurse her indignation in her own room.

Then in came Harvey, dragging a large basket. With the assistance of one of the men servants, he hung upon the tree a quantity of useful articles, shawls, tippets, hoods, and even bonnets, for the girls, — for the little ones, dolls and other toys; for the boys, hats, caps, comforters, " red, white, and blue," skates, tops, balls, &c., — the whole tree ornamented by small flags, the beloved " stars and stripes." Then the colored wax tapers were carefully arranged so as not to endanger the tree when they were lighted.

Books were too heavy for the bending branches of the hemlock; so they were placed on a table near by, a goodly quantity of them, by goodly men and women, who had done their best to please and instruct the " rising generation." *Rising* to what? To be better men and women than their fathers and mothers? *Quien sabe?* Who knows?

The arrangements had all been completed to Harvey's satisfaction; and just as the sun was setting on Christmas eve, he was standing before the beautiful tree with Aunty Dotty, for he had summoned her from her room.

With her arms akimbo, and her thin lips drawn into a condemning sneer, she too surveyed the gorgeously bedecked spruce, and then said, —

" Now, Harvey, I do declare you have been very extravagant. The fruit on that tree must have cost more than a hundred dollars; and the books

on that table another hundred. 'A woful waste
will make a woful want.'"

"But, Aunty Dotty, it is not a waste; they are
all useful articles, except here and there a basket
of candies and a sprinkling of oranges," replied
Harvey, in a mild, conciliatory tone.

"And what do you say to the colored wax tapers
all burning out for just a piece of folly? No such
waste was ever thought of in my time."

"What do you think of the thousands of bright
tapers in the night sky? Are they of any use to
us, besides being beautiful? What's the use of
flowers, and the splendid feathers of birds, or the
delicate colors of sea-shells? Are they not all for
our pleasure? So it is with the tapers to light up
the tree and make it beautiful, to give pleasure to
the school children. Seldom do they enjoy anything of this kind. Come, Aunty, now be reasonable. Put on your best silk gown, and distribute
the gifts to the girls. I am sure it will be a pleasant task. I will do the same for the boys."

"Now, Harvey, you always find a way to get
round me, and make me do as you like. I suppose
I must take a part in this mummery."

So saying, Aunty Dotty left the hall, and very
soon returned, arrayed in a red and yellow changeable silk, that had descended to her as a sort of
heirloom in the family of the Trigs. She wore
about her neck a string of gold beads, that might

have come from Amsterdam centuries ago, for on the mother's side she was of the Vanderthuysens, or Van something else.

Aunty Dotty had one remarkable peculiarity. Like the late Lord Dudley and Ward, of English notoriety, she spoke out what was in her mind, without the least regard to the persons about her. For example: Lord Dudley was one day driving in his carriage through the streets of London. He met an acquaintance, and stopping the carriage, invited the gentleman to take a seat beside him. The invitation was accepted, and they drove on. After some conversation, Lord Dudley relapsed into silence for a few moments, and then said to himself, aloud, " I suppose I shall have to ask this man to dinner." The gentleman said to himself, aloud, " If his lordship should invite me to dinner, I should be obliged to decline."

Now, Miss Dorothy Trig had this same habit.

The children were assembled in the large parlor, before the tree was lighted. When they had all arrived, and had disposed of their wrappings, they were shown into the saloon. Hundreds of wax tapers illuminated the tree. It was a beautiful sight, and the children were as much surprised and delighted as they could have been with the gorgeous palace of Aladdin. Then a band of music in the entrance hall struck up a familiar air, and teachers and children sang a Christmas carol.

7

Clarence and his sister Lucy kept themselves quite in the background, till Harvey, discovering them, brought them forward where they could have a better view.

After the singing ceased, the whole company, as if by a preconcerted arrangement, simultaneously clapped their hands and shouted with all their might.

When the noise subsided, the distribution of the gifts began.

Miss Dorothy, with a long pole in her hand, could reach to the topmost branches.

It so happened that her eyes fell upon Lucy as she stood beside her brother.

" O," said Aunty Dotty, " I must give Lucy Paverley something nice, for she's a good girl, and helps her mother; quite a pretty girl, too; so here's a bright plaid shawl for her." So saying, she brought down the shawl, which was tied up with a blue ribbon in a roll, as it hung on a lower branch of the tree.

Lucy's color rose at this complimentary speech, and she received the gift without being able to utter a word.

" She don't like the shawl. I wonder why!" said Aunty Dotty.

" O, I do like it, very much, indeed," Lucy replied, as Clarence untied the ribbon, and said, " What a pretty thawl!"

" Thawl!" echoed Aunty Dotty, in a contemptuous tone.

" Come, aunty, they are waiting for you," said Harvey.

The distribution continued, Miss Dorothy making her remarks as she went on, till all the gifts for the girls were distributed.

Harvey then supplied the boys with theirs.

To Clarence he gave Sparks's " Life of Franklin ; " and as he did so, he whispered in his ear, —

" If you will learn to speak the letter S, as well as you have the R, I will give you a cow."

Clarence was so much amused with the singular gift thus promised, that he laughed heartily, — the first genuine, hearty laugh he had enjoyed since he left school.

" Thilly-boy," said Aunty Dotty, loud enough for Clarence to hear it.

With perfect good nature, he whispered to Harvey, " Dolly-boy, or little Wainbow, they did call me, you know. Thilly-boy ith a new name."

" I am glad you don't mind what Aunty Dotty says ; she's queer, you know."

A bountiful table was spread in the dining-room ; and thither, led by Aunty Dotty, teachers and scholars hied to partake of the Christmas supper.

When the children had done ample justice to the bountiful supply of substantials and " goodies," Harvey said, —

" Now we will adjourn to the parlor ; and before we part we will sing another Christmas hymn."

Harvey seated himself at the piano, and played an air suitable for the hymn, and teachers and children raised their happy voices together in singing, " While shepherds watched their flocks by night."

For an hour longer they frolicked on the brilliantly lighted lawn.

On their return home, thousands of the lamps of heaven shed down their glittering light upon the happy children, each clasping closely his Christmas gift, and chatting, as they went, on the pleasures of this memorable evening.

Clarence asked his sister if she heard the droll promise Harvey made about his lisping.

" No," she replied, " I did not. What a beautiful thing it is for such a man to have money ! "

" Man ! " exclaimed Clarence ; " he ith but a boy. He wouldn't like to be called a man. He promithed, if I would leave off lithping, to give me a cow."

Here Clarence quite startled Lucy by bursting into a laugh, which rung out loud and clear upon the silent air of night.

" Yeth ; and he even thent Pete a book, a thplendid copy of Robinthon Crutho, with ever tho many engraviugth. Do you know that queer woman called me Thilly-boy ? And what ith worth, I heard thome of the children whithpering it to each other, afterwardth."

" Well, brother, I will help you to learn to speak

the S. We will begin by reading the Life of Franklin in the evenings; and you must try to earn the cow."

"I care leth for the cow than I do for being called Thilly-boy. I am not thilly."

Lucy's face was not visible, or Clarence might have seen that she was stifling a laugh. She did not reply to him for some moments. At length she said, —

"No, brother, you are not silly; but this unfortunate defect in your speech makes you appear so; and it is quite time for you to overcome it. But here we are, at home; and mother has been sitting up for us."

Mrs. Paverley was sleepy and tired with waiting for her children's return; and when they entered the cottage, chatting merrily, she exclaimed, fretfully, —

"Hoity-toity! you don't mind my sitting here alone till this time o' night!"

"I am sorry, mother; but see what our Christmas gifts are," said Lucy, unrolling the thick woollen plaid shawl. "You can wear it, mother, whenever you please."

"And here's a new book for Peter, and lots of cakes and candies. And I am to have a cow one of theth dayth," said Clarence, with a hearty laugh.

"Well, now that is a funny Christmas present. I don't wonder you laugh; and I am glad to hear

you ; for it's the first time since you was a little bit
of a thing, not higher than my knee. Now we'll
go to bed."·

CHAPTER XVI.

UNWELCOME FRIENDS.

THE plaid shawl was worn the next day by Lucy,
although she urged her mother to wear it ; and, accompanied by Clarence, she walked to church.

It was one of those sparkling days of winter,
when the snow seems to reflect the blue of the sky,
and the shadows lying upon that pure snow are almost purple. Dark evergreens lifted their tall spires
heavenward, and the spreading oaks and elms made
a delicate and beautiful tracery upon the clear sky.

Lucy, though poor in purse, was not poor in
mind. What was genuine sentiment in one so
humble and so natural, might have appeared senti-
mentality in a city-born and city-bred miss in her
teens, who had derived all her knowledge of nature
from poetry and romance.

" Isn't there something quite heavenly in the
pretty sky, to-day, Clarence? And the snow in
its purity reminds me of the 'beauty of holiness.'"

Clarence cast a look of surprise at his sister, but
did not answer her question.

" We ought to be very thankful to-day for so many blessings. I enjoy having you with me so much, so much! You are more gentle and kind than Pete."

" Then you think me a *gentle*man," said Clarence, smiling.

" I think in time you will become a good, useful man — a better man than you would have been if you had been indulged in every luxury, as you were with Mrs. Rose, and was in danger of being nothing but a vain, silly dandy."

" But you don't know what a dreadful change it ith for me," the boy exclaimed, with tears starting to his eyes. " I couldn't bear it, if it wathn't for you."

" In time you will confess it was all for the best. But here we are, near the church door, and we will try to make this the best Christmas we have ever known. With all our poverty and needs, we are not so poor as that blessed Saviour who was cradled in a manger, and afterwards had ' not where to lay his head.' "

When the services of the church were over, Lucy and Clarence, thoughtful and solemnized, were walking quietly on the road homeward, when a horse and sleigh, driven rapidly, caused them to jump aside from the beaten path. Indeed, Clarence came very near being run over.

Though the bells on the horse were as many as

he well could carry, above the merry jingling came
a shout, "Hulloa, Dolly-boy."

"O, goodneth me!" exclaimed Clarence; "that
wath Jack — Jack Jimthon; and I think Stackpole
Clap wath the other boy. I wonder where they
are going."

"To the Lindens," said Lucy. "See, they have
stopped at the great gate."

Harvey, who had lingered a while at the church,
now joined Lucy and Clarence.

"Did you see who was in that sleigh?" he inquired. "They passed me so rapidly, I could not
quite make them out; but I think I recognized
Jack Jimson."

"And Stackpole was the other boy," said Clarence.

"Unwelcome as they are, I must make the best
of it, and treat them civilly. Come home with me
to dinner, Clarence."

"*No, I thank you,*" replied Clarence, with an en-
ergy of expression quite startling to Lucy; and
Harvey said, laughingly, —

"No wonder you don't like the company; but I
must say good by, and hurry home to receive those
fellows. I am quite sure Aunty Dotty won't give
them a hearty welcome."

Sure enough. When Harvey, after hastening up
the avenue, had reached the front of the house,
there sat Stackpole Clap in the sleigh, while his

companion, Jack, was talking in a loud voice to some one within the door.

"Say, now, where shall I put my horse? I shall wait here till Harvey comes home."

"You'd better drive off your horse, and go where you came from. We don't have company Christmas day. We had enough last night." This was the shrill voice of Aunty Dotty, who was holding a parley through the keyhole of a closed door with Jack Jimson.

"O, here you are, my dear Harvey!" exclaimed Stackpole, "in time to prevent our being rudely driven from your door."

"Old fellow, how are you?" cried Jack, as he sprung down the flight of steps; and, seizing the hand of Harvey, he gave it such a grip that Harvey fairly winced under it.

"They won't let us in to your hospitable mansion," continued Jack. "What sort of a Cerberus do you keep here?"

"I'll send a servant to take charge of your horse. He seems in need of care, for he is quite in a foam. Come in, boys."

Harvey could not do otherwise than be civil to his quondam schoolmates.

Jack Jimson wore a green shade over one eye, which entirely concealed the swollen, discolored eyelid; for the eye itself was closed, no more to open upon earth.

Aunty Dotty was too much displeased to preside at the dinner-table, and the boys had it all to themselves.

"What a splendid place this is!" said Stackpole. "Who would have thought you were the owner? I should have been as mad as fire, if I had been you, to be called "Old Grayskin.""

"It didn't hurt me," was the calm reply.

"Who do you think we saw, as we were driving along the road? Little Dolly-boy! Not now rigged out in style, but as plain and homely in dress as—"

"As myself," laughingly interrupted Harvey.

"Yes. But you can afford to dress splendidly," exclaimed Jack, "and I suppose he can't. He's as poor as Job's cat."

"He is not to blame for that," calmly replied Harvey.

Jack was nonplused, and made no reply. Stackpole, in a sneaking, snivelling tone, said,—

"I thuppothe he trieth hith beth to keep up acquaintanth with you."

"He makes no effort of that kind," was the curt answer.

"You don't pretend that a fellow of your sense and spirit makes a companion of such a stupid jackass as Clarenth Wothe," retorted Jack, with a malicious sneer.

"You would oblige me, boys, by dropping this

subject. Let me help you to another joint of *turkey*. I think you have a special liking for turkeys."

"Now, that's an insinuation I shouldn't have expected from you, Harvey Amadore," cried Jack, reddening with anger, and throwing down the knife and fork which he had been plying most vigorously, while cramming in the relishing Christmas dinner Aunty Dotty had ordered.

"Come, Jack, don't be vexed; have your plate changed, and try some of this chicken pie."

"There's rhyme and reason in that," said Jack, recovering himself, and handing his plate to the waiter.

"Why, you live like a prince," said Stackpole, in that mean, toadying manner which always disgusted Harvey Amadore. "I shouldn't think you'd want to come back to old Warren's."

"I am very much attached to Mr. Warren, and hope to pass another year with him."

"And then I suppose you will go to college."

"I am not going to college."

"Not going to college!" exclaimed Jack and Stackpole in the same breath.

"No, I am not."

"Well, you are going to try the *otium cum dignitate*, and live like a gentleman," said Jack, spouting out the Latin phrase with astounding emphasis.

"I intend to be a farmer," answered Harvey, coolly.

"A farmer? You are joking," retorted Stack-pole.

"I am in sober earnest. But here comes Aunty Dotty's dessert — mince pies, of course."

"And other things to match," said Jack, rolling his one eye around upon the "goodies." "But where's your wine, Harvey?"

"Aunty and I go for temperance."

"But give us at least a bottle of champagne," said Jack.

"I haven't such an article in the house."

"Now, that's real mean, I say, when you can so well afford it," was the rude remark of bully Jimson, to which Harvey deigned no reply.

"You haven't asked how we happened to be here to-day," said Stackpole, willing to change the subject.

"No. How did it happen?"

"We're on a spree. Jack lives twenty miles off from this place. I am spending part of my holidays with him. So this morning we saw a fine horse and a new sleigh standing before the tavern. Says Jack, 'Suppose we jump in, and take a drive, and I'll pay all expenses.' So we tumbled in, and drove here like the mischief."

"But what will the owner say, when he misses his horse and sleigh? I am afraid you will get into trouble, even if you do pay for the use of them," said Harvey.

"He may whistle for his pay," said Jack. "He will be at the tavern all day, carousing and playing cards, and by the time he wants to go home we shall be there."

"A very bad spree, as you call it. Let me advise you to hasten home," said Harvey, gravely.

"I see you want to get rid of us as soon as possible, Mr. Amadore. Order my horse to the door, if you please," angrily blurted out Jack Jimson.

"Where does Clarenth Wothe live?" inquired Stackpole, with a malicious grin.

"About half a mile from this place; but I hope you don't intend paying him a visit," anxiously replied Harvey.

"I shall do what I please about that, without asking your leave," said Jack, tossing back his head like a vicious horse, and regarding Harvey spitefully with his one eye.

The equipage was soon at the door. Jack, having obtained more direct information, with regard to the dwelling-place of Clarence, of the man who held his horse, threw him a sixpence, and drove off, making a haughty bow to Harvey, who stood upon the door-step, anxiously watching to see what direction the two scamps would take.

CHAPTER XVII.

A SHOWER BATH.

WHEN Clarence heard the sleigh-bells approaching the cottage, he suspected his quondam schoolmates were coming to pay him a visit. Hastily he retreated to his small bedroom, took up a book, and told his sister to say he was engaged, and could not see them.

Soon the horse was stopped, and Stackpole, getting out of the sleigh, rapped loudly at the door.

"Is Clarenth Wothe at home?" asked Stackpole rudely of Lucy, who opened the door.

"If you mean my brother, he is at home; but he is engaged at present, and cannot see you," said Lucy, in her own gentle, sweet manner.

"Haw, haw, haw!" shouted Jack, with his usual loud horse-laugh. "So Dolly-boy is still trying to play the gentleman. That's too ridiculous."

Mrs. Paverley was not at home, and Lucy, not knowing how else to defend herself from their impertinence, closed and locked the door.

"Take up that stick of wood and give a rousing thump on the old door," said Jack to his companion.

Stackpole obeyed his master, for such indeed was Jack to him.

"So you thought you'd take a shower bath this warm day."
Page 111.

Peter now sprang from the settle where he had been seated, and without considering his lameness, seized a bucket of water, and suddenly opening the door, threw the contents of the bucket over Stackpole, drenching him from head to foot; and then the door was quickly closed and locked again.

Stackpole stood shivering and shaking, while the merciless Jack laughed tremendously at the misfortune of his so-called *friend*.

So completely were they occupied with what was going on at the cottage, that the runaway boys did not notice the stealthy approach of a large sleigh with a pair of horses without bells. Two stout men were in the sleigh. One of them sprang out when at a short distance from Jack, and stepping up to the boy, who was laughing at Stackpole, seized him by the shoulder, calling him a " thief," with oaths that need not be repeated.

" So you thought you'd take a shower-bath this warm day," shouted the other man to the dripping Stackpole.

The man who had seized Jack by the shoulder was the owner of the horse and sleigh which the boys had stolen; and he now jumped in beside Jack, and seizing the reins, drove off at full speed.

Meantime, the other man ordered Stackpole to get into the larger sleigh with him; and when the shivering Stackpole obeyed, the man humanely wrapped him in a buffalo skin, saying, with a laugh,

" If I didn't do this you would have an ice-coat on
before the end of the journey. Now you can take a
sweat. Sam Thurston, the owner of yonder horse
and sleigh, said he'd make the runaways sweat for it."

"It was all his doings, Jack Jimson's. I never
should have thought of such a thing if it hadn't been
for Jack; and he promised to pay all expenses."

Just as it might have been expected, the mean,
cringing Stackpole threw all the blame upon his
companion.

Such is the friendship between men and boys of
base, degraded minds and hearts.

The drive of twenty miles was far from an agreeable one; and when the man who carried Jack to
his home gave in his bill for the use of the horse
and sleigh, the father was astonished at the amount;
but fearing his son might receive some worse punishment if he refused, he paid it, hoping that he
should be able to induce Stackpole to pay a part of it.

When that forlorn individual arrived, about half
an hour after Jack, it was quite late; and poor
Stackpole was so exhausted that he could scarcely
move. The man was obliged to lift him out and
carry him into the house.

When it was explained to Mrs. Jimson that the
boy had been drenched with cold water, and afterwards had a drive of twenty miles on a freezing
day, she was seriously alarmed, and a warm bed
and warm tea were prepared for him.

When he was thus made comfortable, Mrs. Jimson went to the room where he was, and inquired how he felt, and whether she should send for a physician.

" I don't want a doctor," was the reply; "he would have to be paid. I am not going to be sick, and I won't take nasty medicine."

" I hope you are not going to be ill," said Mrs. Jimson, kindly.

" Jack got me into all this trouble. I shouldn't have thought of taking the sleigh if he hadn't proposed it. And going to see that contemptible fellow, Clarence Rose, was his doing, and is the reason why I almost got my death of cold."

Contemptible! Who was contemptible now? Mean, sneaking Stackpole Clap.

Boys generally detest meanness. A generous, noble spirit, in youth, has been a distinguishing trait in the character of all truly great men. You would as soon expect a stunted mountain-cedar to grow up into a noble, far-spreading elm tree, as for a mean *boy* to become a generous, benevolent *man.*

No, indeed. Mean boys make hatefully mean men. Some become niggardly misers, and some servile politicians, instead of honest statesmen; others, sneaking pettifoggers, instead of honorable lawyers. The germ of character manifests itself early in life.

8

Now, Stackpole Clap was what Shakespeare calls a " sneakup." He was always ready to join in any diversion, or feast, when other boys were to pay the cost. He was always the retainer or hanger-on of the strongest boy in the school, because he was a coward. He tried to be the companion of the most popular boys, because he had no admirers of his own ; and he courted the rich boys, because he could not appreciate worth that could not be counted in dollars and cents.

Jack Jimson was a fighting bully, a bad fellow ; but he was at this time a pink in comparison with Stackpole Clap, in the estimation of noble-hearted boys, though, in fact, the tendencies of his character were more dangerous.

Mrs. Jimson left the room, which she had entered to comfort and cheer the sufferer, utterly disgusted with the boy ; and unhappy as she was at the misconduct of her own son, she was thankful that he was not like that ungrateful cub whom Jack. had allowed to be his companion. This was quite natural to a mother, and with a mother's tender feeling she thought the father quite severe upon Jack, after she had made the comparison between the two boys.

Yet she was mistaken. Mr, Jimson was not too severe. He paid a large sum to the owner of the horse and sleigh, and deprived Jack of pocket-money for half a year. Moreover, he sentenced him to be shut up in a small room in the fourth story for a month, to be spent in entire solitude, supplied with his ordinary food and an abundance of good books. He was not allowed to see Stackpole, even to bid him good by.

That miserable fellow recovered in a few days, and was sent home, to pass there the remainder of the holidays. A letter of advice from Mr. Jimson to Mrs. Clap, who was a widow, the boy carried home with him, and delivered it to his mother. Bitterly she wept over that letter, for Stackpole was her only child, and she had made a great sacrifice in sparing him from home to give him an education. She was, however, in comfortable circumstances, and there was no reason in the world why Stackpole should be such an unmitigatedly mean fellow.

CHAPTER XVIII.

STRONG MEN.

AFTER Harvey returned to school, he wrote to his excellent guardian, Mr. Hosea Fenton, describing Clarence Rose, his early education, and the character that had been induced by it, and asking advice about what he, Harvey, should do for his friend. In a short time he received the following letter : —

Mr. Hosea Fenton to Harvey Amadore : —

NEW YORK, January 10, 18—.

MY DEAR HARVEY: Your frank and confidential letter of the 6th inst. was duly received. In reply, I give you the best advice of which I am capable.

In our great republic we need strong men — men of physical strength, men of mental strength, men of moral strength. You know boys are to be educated with reference to their manhood. Your young friend is effeminate. More's the pity. We have an abundance of such weak timber — mere willow saplings. We want "hearts of oak." We want real Spartans.

I would not have our sickly children carried away to caverns to die, or drowned in the ocean; but I would have strict attention paid to their physical development.

You know that the Spartan boys were sent to school, when they were no more than seven years old, to be taught how to wrestle and be brave at fisticuffs, so that they might make first-rate fighters. They were educated to be mere soldiers; that was unwise, wrong.

You know the Spartan urchins wore the same clothing, as to warmth, summer and winter. They lay on hard beds, and they often had to go without their dinner.

Now, this last I don't approve of; but I do approve of temperance, strict temperance in food and drink. None of your gluttons or guzzletonians for me. Parents are greatly to blame who allow their children to cloy their appetites with cakes, sweetmeats, and confectionery. Weak stomachs are the consequence, and flaccid muscles, and sappy heads.*

You know how the Spartan boys were flogged, half out of their lives, to learn how to bear pain. Nay, they were sometimes beaten to death without uttering a groan. The Spartan mothers must have been rather hard-hearted—very different, indeed, from the too soft-hearted mothers of our day, or they would have raised an awful outcry against such cruel proceedings.

We need Athenian refinement to soften down Spartan hardihood.

Better far the Christian hardihood like that of the apostle Paul. He made "that determined, almost proud resolve, ' I will not be brought under

---

* " A certain degree of selfishness is likely to be somehow developed in children, for sin of every kind is selfish; but the lowest, meanest, and most utterly degraded type of selfishness is the sensual—that which centres in the body, and makes everything bend to bodily sensation. And yet the early feeding and growth of children tend—how often!—to just this, and nothing higher. * *

" This training he will quite seldom or never outgrow; on the contrary, it will overgrow him, and subjugate all nobler impulses in him. Kindness, it may be, has done it; but it is that kindness which is better called cruelty. Coarseness of feeling, lowness of impulse, gluttony, dissipation, drunkenness,—all foul passions that kennel in a sensual soul,—it has cherished as a foster-mother."

HORACE BUSHNELL.

the power of any.' Under the body? No; he
will scorn that low kind of thraldom. Meats,
drinks, appetites? None of these shall have the
mastery over him. He will assert the supreme
right of the soul, or person, above the house it lives
in; so, God's preëminent right in the soul."

How else could Paul have endured such terrible
physical suffering? He says, "Of the Jews five
times received I forty stripes save one; thrice was
I beaten with rods; once was I stoned; thrice I
suffered shipwreck; a night and a day have I been
in the deep; in weariness and painfulness; in
watchings often; in cold and nakedness."

Brave, heroic St. Paul! Never would he have
become "Paul the aged," if his early life had not
rendered him strong in body to endure such a fearful amount of physical suffering. His trade as a
tent-maker had strengthened his muscles.

Much is said in these days about muscular training. Dumb-bells may do well enough for those who
haven't a chance to swing an axe, and wooden clubs
for those who haven't the opportunity to handle the
spade and the plough. I contend it is better to
harden the muscles by labor, which has a useful result, than that which is merely beating the air.
Yet gymnastics are good in their place.

You will best subserve the true interest of your
friend by leaving him, at present, in the station of
life to which God has called him. If he has talents

for some other station, they will be, in time, developed. President Lincoln was not designed to be all his life a rail-splitter. David, the shepherd boy, was not always to be a keeper of sheep.

Say to your friend, in the strong language of a modern author, " Your life is a school, exactly adapted to your lesson, and that to the best, last end of your existence. No room for a discouraged or a depressed feeling therefore is left you. If your sphere is outwardly humble, if it even appears to be quite insignificant, God understands it better than you do, and it is a part of his wisdom to bring out great sentiments in humble conditions, great characters under great adversities and heavy loads of encumbrance. The tallest saints of God will often be those who walk in the deepest obscurity, and are even despised or quite overlooked by man. Whatever you have laid upon you to do or to suffer, whatever to want, whatever to surrender; or to conquer, is exactly best for you.

" Away, then, with all feeble complaints, all meagre and mean anxieties. Understand, also, that the great question here is not what you will get, but what you will become. The greatest wealth you can ever get will be in yourself. Take your burdens, and losses, and wrongs, if come they must and will, as your opportunities, knowing that God has girded you for greater things than these."

Your friend is fond of dress. He will then inevitably have a craving for money, to gratify his taste for finery, and other luxuries, and for show of all kinds. This must be crushed out. Alas! extravagance is the insatiable monster gnawing at the very vitals of our community. For the attainment of wealth what immense efforts are made, what awful sacrifices endured! The King of Dahomey, · who revels in murder and every abominable crime, is said to be intensely fond of dress. Savages generally are so. *It is said*, too, to be a feminine weakness. A man, a whole-souled, noble man, should despise such weakness in himself. To be neat in person, and dressed according to fitness, — that is, the station in life and the means, — is absolutely required of every man. Effeminate fops, with diamond rings and delicate white kid gloves, are not the kind of beings we need in our republic.

While laboring with the hands faithfully, your friend can still go on with the cultivation of his mind. He may make that his recreation at odd times. This is needed to counteract the other influence — I mean of strengthening the muscles. We don't want gladiators, prize-fighters, pugilists. We want the *mens sana in corpore sano.*

Moreover, and above all, we want good, strong Christian men — men of strong will to do right, in subjection to the will of God — men of integrity — that is, whole, out-and-out Christians, better in every respect as men and citizens, because they are Christians. " More has always been done for God and man by acts than by words."

And another of my favorite authors says, that "the greatness or smallness of a man is, in the most conclusive sense, determined for him at his birth, as strictly as it is determined for a fruit, whether it is to be a currant or an apricot. Education, favorable circumstances, *resolution*, and *industry* can do much; in a certain sense they do *everything;* that is to say, whether the poor apricot shall fall in the form of a green bead, blighted by an east wind, shall be trodden under foot, or whether it shall expand into tender pride and sweet brightness of golden velvet. But apricot out of currant, great men out of small, did never yet art or effort make. The small fruits in their serviceable bunches, the great in their golden isolation, have, the one no cause for regret, nor the other for disdain."

And now, my dear Harvey, you must pardon me for taxing you with so long an epistle. Show it to your friend if you think best. Aid him in every way with money, advice, and, above all, example; but let him remain with his family; there is the place for him at present; and, above all, *let him help himself.*

"Let us, then, be up and doing,
   With a heart for any fate,
Still achieving, still pursuing,
   Learn to labor and to wait."

Faithfully your friend,

HOSEA FENTON.

Harvey enclosed his guardian's letter in one of his own, and sent it to Clarence.

Harvey's own letter was as follows : —

My Dear Clarence :   You will find enclosed Mr. Hosea Fenton's letter of good advice.   We boys don't much relish advice, and yet we need it now as much as we needed the rod when we were toddling youngsters.   I remember the tinglings of the rod, and am sure the smart did me good ; so advice sometimes makes us smart, but we ought to profit by it.

My good guardian is a plain-spoken, honest man, and I trust you will not be offended by his frankness.·

I send you the " Life of Stevenson," the famous inventor of steam carriages, and another volume entitled " Lives of Eminent Mechanics."   You will find that many of the men, who became useful and distinguished, had to surmount immense obstacles.

I have not much school news to communicate.

Mr. Warren found Stackpole Clap such a disagreeable member of our family circle that he was obliged to send him home.   After his return to school, instead of being better for the loss of his crony, Jack Jimson, he became much worse than formerly in endeavoring to imitate Jack ; he beat the copy, as we say ; not in daring, but in insolence. He was excessively impertinent to Mrs. Warren, and tormented and embarrassed me, by being a constant hanger-on and an egregious flatterer.

We are all glad to be freed from his intensely disagreeable presence. I am very sorry for his mother, for I am told she does not know what to do with her troublesome son.

Have you conquered the S, as you did the R? In this, as in many other things, *C'est le premier pas qui coûte — Perseverantia vincit omnia.*

Don't call me a pedant !

I expect to be at home before many weeks. Mr. Warren advises me to go to —— College ; not for the whole academical course, but for the scientific department alone. A knowledge of chemistry, mineralogy, geology, &c., he says, is very important for a farmer.

Remember me kindly to your mother and sister, and believe me, Clarence,

Truly your friend,
HARVEY AMADORE.

CHAPTER XIX.

CONQUERING DIFFICULTIES.

THE latter part of the winter of 18— was very severe. In consequence of Pete's lameness, Clarence was obliged to do all the out-door work, and to wait upon his brother in many ways — very trying to one who had always been accustomed to be waited upon himself. Although so weary when evening closed in, that he was in danger of falling asleep, he became interested in the books furnished by Harvey, and listened while Lucy or his brother read aloud.

It was a great source of mortification to Clarence that Peter could read out better than he could, because his brother did not lisp, and had a good, strong voice.

Peter had been to school only two winters; yet he had learned to read well and to write a tolerable hand: he had, besides, made some advance in arithmetic, and now set about improving himself with a zeal which quite astonished Clarence, and stimulated him to exert himself.

When the wintry storm howled about the cottage, and the snow was driven furiously against the windows, the scene within was bright and cheery.

The stove sent forth its genial warmth. Two tallow candles on the pine table did not make a brilliant light, but it was quite sufficient for the readers.

Mrs. Paverley was employed with her knitting, and Lucy with sewing, while Pete read out to them. Clarence, to keep himself awake, set about whittling a winding-reel and a work-box for his sister.

This was a fine time for softening down the roughness of Pete's character.

As for Clarence, he was thriving on plain diet and hard work. He began to grow amazingly, both in height and breadth. His narrow chest was expanding, and his shoulders becoming broad. He cried only now and then, when his fingers ached cruelly, or the tips of his ears were frozen. Who wouldn't cry under such circumstances, excepting, always, those tough-skinned, wonderful Spartan boys?

Clarence was taking lessons of his sister in elocution. Like Demosthenes, he had a great difficulty to be overcome in the art of speaking. He did not, like that famous orator, put pebbles in his mouth, nor roar to the sea till he was himself as hoarse as the waves dashing against a rocky coast. He hissed and sissed, keeping his teeth tightly shut to hold his tongue in, until at last he could say *sister* — the first word he uttered without lisping; and it ought to have been, for Lucy had taken unwearied pains with him to conquer this defect in his speech.

Glad was Clarence when the winter was over, and showery April, the month of smiles and tears, was renovating the earth and clothing it with a new verdant mantle.

One sunny day, a face as sunny and bright was heartily welcomed at the cottage.

" I am right glad to *see* you, Harvey," said Clarence, laying a strong emphasis upon the " see."

Harvey smiled, made no remark upon the success thus achieved, but replied, —

" Thank you. I find you are busy this morning ; a fine morning for gardening."

Clarence was digging in the small garden attached to the cottage.

" Do·you think you will like gardening?" inquired Harvey, in a manner showing he attached importance to the answer.

" Yes. I shall like it better than anything I have had to do since I left *cool* (correcting himself, and coloring) — since I left school."

Then throwing down his spade, he asked Harvey to go in and see his mother and sister.

Harvey declined, saying he had a pressing engagement, to which he must give immediate attention.

About two hours after Harvey left, Clarence was still digging in the garden. Pete had just returned from the village where he had carried the week's washing, and was putting Patchy into the small stable. A man appeared on the road driving a small white cow and a calf, which frisked in its own awkward fashion beside its mother.

" What a beautiful cow ! " exclaimed Pete.

" Is this Mrs. Paverley's ? " cried the man, from the road.

" It is," shouted Pete, while Clarence threw down his spade, approached the man, and looked anxiously at the two animals.

"Here's a bit of paper will 'splain all about the cow and calf. Where shall I drive 'em ? " said the man.

Now, Pete had never heard of Harvey's promise to Clarence, and was utterly astonished when his brother, after glancing at the note, said, —

" Drive them into the barn."

The note contained these few words :

CLARENCE : You have conquered ! One conquest is a sign of more. The cow and calf are yours, honestly won. Truly your friend,

HARVEY.

Clarence was moderately pleased, but Pete's joy knew no bounds. He proved the recovered strength of his ankle by jumping up and down, and the strength of his lungs by shouting at the top of his voice, " Hurrah ! hurrah ! What an *elegant* cow ! "

Like many persons more refined than himself, Pete did not understand the right use of the epithet " elegant " — a word, the true signification of which seems not to be well understood in some parts of our country, where they speak of elegant butter, elegant potatoes, and an elegant pig! Webster defines elegant — "delicately refined, graceful, pleasing to taste."

If the cow was elegant, and the calf too, in the vocabulary of Pete, so was not Pete himself, according to the venerable lexicographer.

He, Pete, turned two or three summersaults, stood on his head, and knocked his feet together, and when he came down on the right end, cut a double-shuffle that could not have been excelled by a Carolina negro. The calf itself might have performed these antics as gracefully.

Clarence was inclined to look very gravely upon the generous gift of his friend Harvey, it not corresponding at all with his notions of elegance; but Pete's ridiculous manifestations of joy quite overcame his gravity, and his hearty laugh was echoed by Lucy, who, on hearing Pete's shouting, had hastened to learn the cause. They were soon joined by the mother, who, if she did not imitate Pete in his manifestations, was equally pleased. With uplifted arms she exclaimed, "I never! I never, never, never!"

"You never owned so pretty a cow, mother," said Clarence. "Well, she is yours. Harvey has given her to me freely, to do with her what I please, and I am delighted to make you a present."

"O, no, no, no!" exclaimed the mother.

"Please don't refuse my gift. And Pete, you may have the calf."

"You think 'like likes its like,' as the old proverb has it," replied Pete with a merry laugh. "I will take care of the thing for you if you'll only give me some hay for Whity. There ain't grass enough on the Common for her yet, and Patchy mustn't be starved entirely."

"I'll provide the hay," said Harvey, pointing to a cart-load of hay which two oxen were drawing into the barn-yard.

"That Harvey Amadore is a whole team himself," exclaimed Pete, again going off into athletic exercises unknown to the practice of any modern gymnasium; and then he climbed to the top of the load, and helped to pitch the hay into the barn.

CHAPTER XX.

FLITTING.

HARVEY consulted with his excellent guardian about the future course he should pursue with regard to Clarence. His advice was very judicious.

Let him become a first-rate gardener; that is, if he is capable of it. Make a trial of his capacity. I was

9

lately at the Lindens. I observed that the cottage formerly occupied by the gardener is now vacant. Suppose you remove the Paverley family to the place. It is not best to separate them. You know how much force there is in the trite motto, "Union is strength." If you don't know it, you ought to know it; and so ought every man and boy in our United States, especially at this time. Well, to the question on the *tapis*. Let the boy you call your friend learn to take charge of your flower garden and pleasure grounds. Let the other boy work on the farm. The mother and daughter can make butter — be dairy women. Give them the opportunity. You can but make the experiment. The older boy, you say, has taste; that is quite requisite for a gardener. Give him an opportunity to cultivate it with reference to gardening. Don't spoil your protégé, Harvey, by making him too refined for his employment.

I could say more on this subject, but for want of time must come to a close.

Truly your friend and guardian,
HOSEA FENTON."

On the 1st of May, the Paverley family were flitting to Linden Hill. The mansion and grounds attached to the place bore the name of "The Lindens." Harvey, with the consent of his guardian, had left school, and had made all the needful arrangements for the removal that was now taking place.

It was for Mrs. Paverley a return to a much-loved home. There she had passed the happiest years of her life with her husband. The very roses, honeysuckles, and clematis now spreading themselves luxuriantly over the whole front and ends of the cottage, and even over the roof, were planted by her husband, who had been the gardener at the Lindens.

The cottage had now been thoroughly repaired, and a nice, cool dairy-room and ice-house had been added to it. It was sufficiently spacious for the accommodation of the family, having four rooms on the ground floor and three finished bedrooms in the attic, besides an open garret-room.

Mrs. Paverley lifted her hands with wonder and delight as she entered the little parlor, exclaiming, as usual, "I never! I never! Who would have thought it?" — while Lucy, though less demonstrative, was equally pleased.

A pretty green and white paper covered the wall; three or four engravings, in walnut frames, hung against it. The chairs and tables were neat, but plain. But what most delighted Lucy was a book-case, a small bookcase, with glass doors, completely filled with books. Time would show how judiciously they were selected. Clarence, at a glance, perceived that many of them were upon gardening, in its various departments.

Harvey had kept himself entirely out of sight

while the moving was taking place. Pete seemed to have the strength of a young giant, as he assisted in handling the heavy boxes and barrels which contained the articles from the kitchen and pantry of the old house, and lifting them from the cart to which Patchy was *attached* (in more senses than one, if close companionship could have had that effect). Patchy was no longer a rack of bones, — prospective crow's meat ; — he was in as good a condition as Pete himself, and almost as full of life and spirit.

Clarence alone showed no signs of joy. The contrast between this pretty cottage and the poor old brown house from which they had removed was not in his mind. He was comparing this small, simple habitation with the fine mansion in which he had passed so many years of petted indulgence. To him, therefore, the change was of small consequence. He was merely enduring the present, and looking forward to the future, when he should once more revel in luxury.

Clarence had carefully kept one cherished secret. Mrs. Rose, on the eve of her departure, wrote to him, assuring him that whenever Mr. Rose should make a fortune, as he expected to do, of course, in that Eldorado, California, she should claim Clarence again as her son. Month after month passed, and not a word for Clarence from Mr. or Mrs. Rose. He much wondered at their silence ; but still hope was the rainbow that cheered him with its brilliant hues — brilliant and evanescent. In his own room tears were still abundant. Whatever he did in the way of work was done in a perfunctory manner; there was no heart in it. Pete, on the contrary, worked with a will. He had never dreamed of living in such a nice cottage, and having a calf of his own. He was as " happy as a lord " — poor comparison that. Pete was as happy as a hearty, active boy, with a cheerful temperament and every real want supplied, need to be. He could not understand why Clarence was not as " raving glad " as Pete said he was himself, when they were settled in the white cottage.

It was the 6th of May. As lovely a twilight as ever cast its golden hues over Eden now fell serenely upon Linden Hill.

The white cottage was about a quarter of a mile from the mansion on the hill, which, from the fine avenue of linden trees, was appropriately called The Lindens.

The labor of setting all " to rights " in the cottage was completed, and the Paverley family were seated in the latticed porch, at the front door. The perfume of violets gladdened the air. The birds were having a charming concert in the neighboring trees, unmindful of the added bass from a solitary bullfrog.

" I say, now," said Pete, " all this seems to me a queer sort of a dream — a very funny one ; and I wonder why I don't wake up and find it so. It's real, though, for there comes Mr. Amadore."

During the removal and until this time Harvey had not made his appearance at the cottage. The family rose at his approach.

"Keep your seats, I beg of you; don't let me disturb you. I will sit upon this step, if you please."

Lucy immediately went in doors, brought out a chair, and placed it upon the grass, near the steps.

"Thank you; since you have taken that trouble, I can't refuse," said Harvey, as he seated himself. "What a perfect evening!" he continued. "I hope, Mrs. Paverley, you find yourself comfortably settled."

"O, Mr. Harvey, we owe you so much!" exclaimed the grateful woman.

"You owe me nothing —"

"No," interrupted Pete, "we don't mean to owe anybody. I expect to work for my living. I don't mean to be a hanger-on to anybody."

"That's the right spirit," said Harvey. "You are not dependent upon me. I expect to pay you wages by the month for your work on the farm, and the same to Clarence for gardening. If Mrs. Paverley and Lucy find the work of the dairy too much for them, I know of a stout woman who can help them."

"No, indeed! We are used to hard work. I was

brought up on a farm, and can make butter as yellow as gold!" said Mrs. Paverley.

"Half the produce of the dairy will belong to you, and the other half goes to the credit of the farm. Will this satisfy you all?"

"Entirely," said the mother. "And what are we to pay for house-rent?"

"This cottage has always been free to the gardener. It is so now, if Clarence agrees to the arrangement."

Harvey did not look at Clarence as he said this; if he had, he might have seen two unbidden tears roll over a pair of flushed cheeks. Alas! they were not tears of gratitude. Pride was throbbing at the heart of the boy, and with a voice half choked, he muttered, —

"Thank you."

Harvey replied, "No thanks to me, Clarence. I expect to have to thank you one of these days. You and Pete have a glorious opportunity for helping yourselves, and becoming strong men through your own exertions. I have often wished that I could do the same, and win my way against wind and tide; but it has not been so ordered," he added, reverently, "and I must try to do the best I can, God helping me, in the position in which he has placed me. But to change the subject somewhat abruptly, if you will come to the Hall to-morrow morning, Clarence, you and your brother, I will make you acquainted with the gardener and the farmer, under whose directions you will, for the present, be placed."

"That I will, after I have taken care of Whity and Pet. You ought to see my calf — how wonderful she has grown in a month. Would you be willing to step to the barn, and look at the pretty creature?"

"Certainly," said Harvey, starting up, ready to follow Pete. "Good evening, Mrs. Paverley; good evening, Lucy. Clarence, will you go with us?"

"No, I thank you; I haven't the same admiration for calves that Pete has."

There was more of the puppy in Clarence than he himself suspected, or than his true friend was willing to believe.

So Harvey and Pete went together to the barn, and Mrs. Paverley and Lucy into the cottage, leaving Clarence to his sulkiness; for sulky he was, rather than sad; dissatisfied with himself, and with everybody else.

Buoyed up he had been through the severe winter, amid all his trials, by the hope of being once more with his indulgent mamma, when he ought to have been grateful for the kind, good mother God had given him — a blessing beyond all price. In her extremity she had parted with him, but she had never ceased to love him, and to pray for him.

The next morning the countenance of Clarence

had assumed a more pleasant expression. How could he resist the influence of such a beautiful morning, when all nature was in holiday garb, rejoicing in the sweet breath and charming melody of the renovating spring?

Though his taste had been perverted by selfishness, and all that was bright and beautiful had been considered mainly, or almost entirely, as means for his personal adornment, yet the boy possessed, as a good gift, taste, which needed cultivation and a right direction.

Earth was not made so beautiful for beasts nor for blind men — morally blind !

As the boys walked rapidly to the Lindens, the thoughts that occupied their minds were widely different.

Pete thought, "What a nice thing to be a farmer!" Clarence thought, "What a miserable lot is mine, to be a gardener! And yet it's better than being a farmer." And so they walked on in silence, till they reached the great gate at the entrance of Linden Hill. There Harvey was waiting for them. He directed Pete to a distant field, where the farmer was planting potatoes.

"Tell him to set you to work," said Harvey.

Pete ran off at full speed, and then Harvey led the way to the garden, accompanied by Clarence. Harvey did not appear to notice the discontented air of his companion. The gardener was a Scotch-

man; a small, gray-headed man, with a shrewd
countenance, and a cheek like "a rose in the snaw."
He was stooping over a bed of hyacinths. As the
two boys approached, he raised himself, and, taking
off his woollen cap, make a nod, rather than a bow.

"Sandy, I have brought the lad I was speaking
to you about. You can teach him gardening."

Sandy closed one eye, and with the other scrutinized Clarence for a full minute.

"But, mon," said he, addressing Harvey, "ken
ye if the lad has the giftie for it?"

"We shall see; we shall see. There's nothing
like trying. What splendid hyacinths!"

The attention of Clarence had been drawn to the
beautiful array of flowers, white, pink, purple, yellow, fresh and dewy, rejoicing in the bright morning sun.

In his button-hole Sandy had a daisy, and Harvey
remarked, "That little flower seems to be a favorite, Sandy."

"And wherefore na'? 'Wee modest, crimson-
tippet flower,' as Bobby Burns called it. Not your
American daisy, the uncanny thing that spoils the
hay in this country. That white-weed is not a
daisy."

Sandy saw that Clarence was admiring the hyacinths heartily, and with a knowing wink to Harvey, whispered, "He'll do."

"I'll leave him with you, Sandy, to show him

your garden and green-house. Good morning, Clarence." So saying, Harvey walked away.

As Sandy turned from the bed of hyacinths, he beckoned to Clarence to follow ; and as Clarence did so, he heard the old man repeating, from his favorite Burns, —

> " To catch Dame Fortune's golden smile,
>   Assiduous wait upon her ;
> And gather gear by every wile
>   That's justified by honor ;
> Not for to hide it in a hedge,
> Not for a train attendant,
> But for the glorious privilege
> Of being independent."

CHAPTER XXI.

ALL IS NOT GOLD THAT GLITTERS.

SPRING had decked the garden at the Lindens with her choicest flowers. Summer, not to be outdone, spread a brighter, gayer tapestry over mother earth, and was almost ready to yield up her reign to Autumn, when Clarence received the following letter : —

SAN FRANCISCO, March 30.

MY DEAR CLARENCE : You must have been troubled by not hearing from us for so long ; but

we had a very long and stormy passage, — seasick
all the way, — and did not arrive till nearly five
months after we left New York, going by the way
of Cape Horn. O, that dreadful voyage! And
now I did hope to send my precious something
pretty from California — at least a fine gold pin, or
a ring; but, Clarence, we are poor. Your papa
has been quite sick ever since we have been here,
and hasn't done any business at all; so that we
are still living on the money we brought with us,
and now that is nearly gone. I don't know what
we shall do when it is all gone, for we have no
relatives or friends here.

I can't think of you without tears, suffering, as
you must be, all the evils of poverty, so delicately
and genteelly brought up as you have been. I did
hope we should be able to send for you to come out
to us; but I give up the hope now, and I am afraid
I shall never see you again.

Your papa sends love, and says, " Tell Clarence
to keep up good courage, and try to make the best
of his situation. A boy with resolution and right
principles can get along well in our country, if he
only has health. Opportunities are never wanting
to those who are ready to make the best use of
them." You must write to me, my darling, and
tell me all about yourself. Have you grown taller?
I hope you haven't lost your pretty complexion. I
should be sorry to see you all sun-burned and coarse-

looking. Don't fail to brush your teeth, and to keep your nails clean. Remember me to your mother. I hope she takes good care of your clothes. It is a comfort to me to think you had nice full suits of all kinds when I left you. I think they must last a good while. And now, darling, I must say good by.

Ever your loving

MAMMA.

Tears and smiles chased each other over the face of Clarence as he read this characteristic letter. He valued the true affection of Mrs. Rose, mingled as it was with her more than womanly weakness. Now the hope he had so fondly cherished of being once more with Mr. and Mrs. Rose, and enjoying the luxuries which had rendered him so effeminate, — that hope was entirely swept away, and he resigned himself to his present condition. Moreover, for the first time, he felt a warm glow of gratitude to Harvey Amadore.

Clarence sought his sister, to tell her about Mrs. Rose. Lucy was busily employed in the dairy, working up the nice, yellow butter into rolls, and stamping them with the American eagle — a design Clarence himself had cut in wood for that purpose.

Lucy saw at once that Clarence had been weeping. Indeed, the briny fountain at the corners of his eyes seemed perennial, and overflowed on the least provocation.

In this case he was excusable; for he really loved Mrs. Rose.

When Lucy had heard the sad news, she was not surprised at her brother's grief.

"What should we have done without Harvey?" exclaimed Clarence. "I intend, now, to work with a will, for I am beginning to like gardening."

"It was man's work when he was in a state of innocence, and it has been the delight of thousands and millions since the fall," said Lucy, with enthusiasm.

"Do you know, Lucy, I mean to make a first-rate gardener? This is my resolution on this my fifteenth birthday."

"It's a splendid resolution. I'll follow it up with another. I mean to make the best dairy-woman in the country. Do you know our butter already sells for the highest price in market?"

"I should think it would, for it is the sweetest, nicest butter I ever put into my mouth. I wish poor mamma had some of it, and a bouquet, too, of our beautiful flowers. But I must go to work; I have already staid too long. By the way, our night-blooming cereus will be out this evening. Will you go with me to the Hall, and see it? Sandy told me to ask you."

"I shall be delighted to go. Good morning."

With an elastic step, and a determined air, Clarence sped over the ground till he reached the garden at the Lindens. The way in which he attacked the weeds in one of the flower-beds, with a small hoe, quite amused Sandy.

" O, mon, I think you handle your hoe this morning so as to put the flowers in danger of their lives. You must suppose you are fighting your foes," said Sandy, leaning on his spade, and looking anxiously after the fate of his dear verbenas.

· " I am fighting my enemies, the weeds," said Clarence, good-naturedly, " and worse enemies still — Pride and Laziness."

" Weel, you'll root them sins out, tough as they are. You've made a right good beginnin'.

> ' What tho' on hamely fare we dine,
> Wear hodden gray, and a' that ;
> Gie fools their silks, and knaves their wine —
> A mon 's a mon for a' that,
> For a' that, and a' that,
> Their tinsel show, and a' that.
> The honest man, though e'er sae poor,
> Is king o' men for a' that.'

Do you know, Master Clarence, that the greatest and wisest king that ever lived was a great botanist? "

" I did not know it. Who was he? "

" Why, Solomon, sure ; he knew plants from the cedar of Lebanon to the moss upon the wall. And David, too, he knew all about the nature of trees. Didn't he compare the good mon to the palm tree, and the bad mon to the poison bay tree. Don't

you remember the beautiful varse in the Psalms that
ends thus, where David speaks of the good mon?—

> ‘He shall be fat and full of sap,
> And aye be flourishing.’ ”

Sandy flourished his spade by way of giving emphasis to this last quotation, and then vigorously
resumed his work.

CHAPTER XXII.

AUNTY DOTTY'S CALL.

AUNTY DOTTY was curious to see the Paverley
family in their new home, and yet she allowed
months to elapse before she paid them a visit at the
gardener's cottage.   At last she made up her mind
to go there, and arrayed herself in that beloved
changeable silk, put on her black satin coal-scoop
bonnet, drew on a pair of long black mitts, and
walked off in as stately a manner as she could possibly assume.

It was just at sunset of a summer evening.   Mrs.
Paverley and Lucy were milking the cows in a little
meadow through which a merry brook rejoiced on
its winding way.   Clarence was lingering at the
Lindens, listening to Sandy's “ wise saws and modern instances.”

As Aunty Dotty drew near the cottage she saw
Pete, who was nailing up a honeysuckle which
threatened to exclude the light entirely from the
front window of the parlor.

"Boy, where's your mother?" said Miss Dotty,
in her blunt way.

"Gone to milking," was the curt reply, in a tone
and manner very like the questioner's.

"I s'pose I must go in and wait for her then."

"I s'pose you must," replied Pete, pointing to the
open door.

Miss Dotty entered, and took a seat in the parlor
near the front window.

It will be remembered that cousin Dotty thought
aloud. Peter overheard her muttering to herself, —

"A smart parlor; too smart by half for poor
folks. Books, too, lots of 'em. I wonder how
they can get time here to read. And picters, too, I
declare. Well, now, if that ain't too much for
patience to bear. Harvey is awful extravagant.
He'll run out the whole property before he's twenty-
five. These folks 'll grow proud, and won't work as
well for being made so fine."

Pete, hearing every word as he stood by the window, was growing more and more wrathy every
minute. At length he could endure no longer in
silence, and blurted out, in no gentle tone, —

"I've worked for my living ever since I was
knee high to a grasshopper, and I expect to earn

10

my living always. I don't mean to be obligated to anybody."

"You needn't be spunky, boy. You know our Harvey fixed up this cottage so smart for you, and that he gives you cows, and calves, and all sorts of things, for nothing."

Mrs. Paverley and Lucy now came to the door with their milk-pails filled to the brim with rich, foaming milk.

"You've got company in there," said Pete, with a scornful laugh.

The pails were placed in the dairy-room, and Mrs. Paverley, putting on a clean apron, and telling Lucy to do the same, soon made her appearance in the parlor.

"You're quite welcome here, Miss Trig," said Mrs. Paverley.

"To be sure I ought to be," replied Miss Dotty; pursing up her mouth and twitching her long, sharp chin. "Who's a better right?"

Mrs. Paverley was too much surprised to answer a word. She seated herself, and waited for her visitor to continue the conversation.

"Your boy is sassy. He spoke up to me right tart just now, there, by that window."

"What, our Peter! I am sorry if he offended you in any way," said Mrs. Paverley, but not in a very humble tone.

"Offended! I wouldn't be offended by such a

young chap, who, I s'pose, hasn't been taught any better manners."

Lucy now came in, her apron white as snow, and her hair neatly arranged. She had been delayed a moment by Peter at the front door, who said he had something to whisper in her ear. While he did so he placed a couple of damask rosebuds within her comb, at the back of her head.

" Smart! Smart! Everything so dreadful smart! Flowers in the hair, to be sure!" muttered Dotty, much to the surprise of Lucy, who could not comprehend the meaning of this odd soliloquy.

" Would you be pleased to take a glass of warm milk?" asked Lucy, in her own sweet, kindly manner.

" No. I don't like warm milk; but I could take some cream and strawberries, too; for I 'spose you have plenty here. We don't get many up at the Hall."

"I will get the cream," said Lucy, " but we have no strawberries. Would you like some biscuits with it?"

" Yes; for I've had a long walk, and didn't take my tea beforehand, because Harvey is coming home to-night, and I wanted to take supper with him."

"I am sorry we haven't a cup of tea to give you; but we have our tea and dinner together at noon, and don't have tea in the evening," said Mrs. Paverley.

Miss Dotty muttered, " They live on the fat of the land. Harvey is spoiling these poor folks entirely."

Lucy returned with a tray, which she placed on a small table before Miss Dotty. The biscuits were light and white as snow; a glass of smooth, yellow cream was beside them, and a few little round radishes Lucy had hastily pulled from her own garden.

Mrs. Paverley now excused herself by saying that she must strain the milk they had just brought in.

While Miss Dotty was applying herself right heartily to the entertainment set before her, Lucy took up a book, seated herself by the front window, and began to read.

The mischievous Pete, stooping underneath the window, whispered, " How do you like your company?"

Lucy shook her head reprovingly.

Nothing daunted, Pete continued, ' Why don't you talk to that hen-turkey?"

Lucy was obliged to change her seat.

" Girl, who made these biscuits?" inquired Miss Dotty, after she had eaten half a dozen of them.

" I made them. I am glad if you like them."

" Well, now, I shouldn't have thought that a gal, who fixed up her hair so mighty fine with posies and curls, would know anything about cooking."

Here a laugh was heard — a real guffaw — from Pete.

Lucy did not understand the allusion to the rose-buds; she civilly replied, —

" My mother has taught me to do all kinds of work."

" But I dare say you like reading better. Novels I s'pose you read, and varses."

" I seldom read a novel; but I am fond of poetry," said Lucy, innocently.

" Not suitable reading for a girl that has to work for a living — puts notions in their heads, and make 'em soft and silly — lovesick, too."

Lucy's cheeks rivalled the roses in her hair, and her forehead was of the same bright hue, as she replied, —

" I hope the poetry I read will not have that effect. This is a volume of Longfellow's poems."

" Now, you don't mean to say that's the name of a poet! I never heard tell of a writer of that name. I've heard of Dr. Watts, and one Cowper, and Joel Barlow's Hasty Pudding, but never of a Long-fellow."

Here another loud laugh came in from beneath the window.

" I do say now, gal, that brother of yourn is the very sassicst limb that ever I met in all my born days. He deserves a good cowhiding, and I'd give it to him if I had a chance. But it's time for me to be going."

So saying, Miss Dotty rose, and making a supercilious nod to Lucy, stalked out of the house. There she was met by Pete, who made her a low, awkward bow, and asked if she would have a cow-hide now; he would get one in the barn; or whether she would wait for another chance.

" Get along with your impartinence. I shall report you to Harvey Amadore, your young master."

" I call no man master, nor boy neither," said Pete, proudly.

Miss Dotty assumed an air of dignity, — mock dignity it was, which commanded no respect, — and as she held up her gown daintily, and stepped off like a blackbird, Pete followed her a few rods, mimicking her in the most complete and laughable manner.

About half an hour after cousin Dotty's departure from the cottage, Harvey returned home. As he was approaching the gate of Linden Hall he saw Pete, leading a young heifer by a rope tied around its neck. Harvey stopped at the gate. The animal seemed to have a will of its own quite in opposition to Pete's will; and to exert it to the utmost. It pulled and tugged one way. He, afraid of hurting the heifer, partly coaxed and partly dragged the other way, occasionally letting the rope loose with one hand, to wipe away tears from his eyes. Pete was not given to much weeping; but this was a hard case. Pete and Pet were friends, and an opposition of this kind was not agreeable to either.

" What is the matter, Peter? What are you going to do with your calf?" inquired Harvey.

" Going to take it where it belongs."

" It belongs to you; but you are leading it a contrary way."

" It don't belong to me. I don't choose to be beholden to anybody."

" I suppose Clarence gave you the calf, and you have a right to it. You have raised it."

" Well, I thought so till a while ago. I don't want to be twitted with being a sort of hanger-on, and having a master.".

" Who has been so unjust as to intimate such a thing?"

" I don't choose to tell; but somebody complains that you will ruin yourself by doing so much for our folks."

" Now, Pete, that is perfectly ridiculous. Are you not working for wages?"

" That I don't mind. I like to work. But I don't like to keep what don't belong to me. Come, Pet, you must go where you belong."

The pretty heifer, tired with its exertions, had lain down on the grass by the road-side.

" Let us reason quietly about this matter, Peter. I offered a cow to Clarence if he would overcome the habit of lisping, which made him appear silly. With a great effort he did so, and fairly earned the reward."

"But you didn't promise him the calf."

"Well, honest Pete, the calf belonged to the cow, and I chose it should go with her. What is the poor thing going to do without its mother?"

"O, it's weaned. See here." And Pete gathered a handful of tender grass, and offered it to the animal, who did not show a very great desire for the food.

"Peter, could you do an extra hour's work on the farm now, at this busy time?"

"Yes, indeed, I could as well as not; an hour in the morning before breakfast."

"Then in a couple of months the calf would be fairly your own; you would have earned it. How do you like the bargain? Would that satisfy you?"

"First rate. Come, Pet, we'll go home." So saying, right about turned Pete, and the calf followed, without the rope, making the most awkward demonstrations of joy at her freedom.

Harvey suspected who had been mischievously intermeddling with his affairs, and that very evening had a long talk with Aunty Dotty, the result of which was, that she must mind her own business, or she would lose the pleasant home she now enjoyed through the kindness and liberality of Harvey's father.

CHAPTER XXIII.

A FAMILY CONSULTATION.

WE now pass over the autumn months, and jump to winter.

The little parlor at the Paverley cottage presented a cheerful appearance one cold evening in the month of December.

It was the first time they had indulged themselves in a fire in that spare room. Now it sparkled and merrily blazed up the chimney. A pair of brass andirons seemed to know the place they had occupied years before, for they shone as brightly as possible, and reflected the pleasant countenances of Mrs. Paverley, Lucy, and Pete.

A small table, on which were several books and a work-box, was drawn up near the fire. Mrs. Paverley, with her knitting, sat on one side of the fireplace, while Lucy and Pete were at the table, Lucy sewing and Pete much engrossed with slate and pencil, " doing sums," as he called it.

" I wonder why Clarence don't come home ; he is later than usual," said Lucy.

Clarence had gone to the neighboring town to make some purchases for the household.

" There he comes, now," said Pete, placing slate

and pencil upon the table, and hastening out to meet and assist his brother.

The horse and wagon were quickly disposed of, and the parcels brought in.

Clarence then came into the parlor, drew a chair near the table, and took a letter from his pocket.

Pete resumed his slate.

As Clarence read the letter, the family saw he was greatly agitated.

The receipt of a letter was an unusual occurrence at the cottage.

"Bad news?" inquired Mrs. Paverley.

"Very bad," was the reply. "Mr. Rose is dead."

"Indeed! And where is Mrs. Rose?"

"In New York. She arrived nearly a month ago. This letter has been lying two or three weeks in the post-office. Mr. Rose died after a long, severe illness, during which nearly all the money he took with him was spent, not leaving enough even to bury him; and poor mamma had to sell her jewelry, and even a part of her wardrobe, to pay her passage home, and the few debts that were due in California."

Here Clarence laid his head upon the table, and burst into a violent fit of weeping.

After a sorrowful silence of some minutes, Lucy gently asked, —

"And where is poor Mrs. Rose now?"

"At the —— Hotel in New York, with not a friend or relation there to assist her. Poor and sick, what will she do?" sobbed out Clarence, without lifting his head from the table.

"Come to us," said Mrs. Paverley.

"Yes, we can take care of her," added Lucy.

"So we can," echoed Pete.

"How kind!" exclaimed Clarence, raising his head and looking at his mother through tears; "how kind for you to propose such a thing!"

"Didn't Mrs. Rose take care of you for more than ten years? What else could we do but offer her a home now, humble one though it must appear to her who has lived so grandly?" said the mother.

"I don't think she'll care for style now," said Pete; "and, besides, I am sure our house is good enough for anybody."

"But can we make her comfortable?" questioned Clarence, anxiously.

"We can try," replied Lucy. "Mother, if you are willing, we will give up this room for Mrs. Rose's bedroom.

"No, Lucy, that is too much of a sacrifice," said Clarence, doubtfully.

"We have no other spare room, Clarence, and we ought to offer the best we have to the poor sick lady. I am thankful that we have it to offer," replied Mrs. Paverley.

"O, mother, how *good* you are!" exclaimed Clarence.

" I was a stranger, and ye took me in," said Pete, with an attempt at solemnity, that, under any other circumstances, would have been irresistibly ludicrous.

" But how can we make this room suitable for a bedroom ? " said Clarence.

" We shall only have to purchase bedstead, bed, and bedding, and a bureau and wash-stand."

" And how can we do all that?" doubtfully suggested Clarence.

" We have some money laid aside from our dairy," said Mrs. Paverley.

" And I have some from my wages," said Pete. " I was wondering what I should do with it; this is a first-rate chance."

" I haven't much, for I spent so much for my winter clothing," added Clarence ; " but I have enough to pay my expenses to New York and back again. So, mother, if you will consent, I will start to-morrow for the city, and bring mamma home."

" Right, my son ; and we will be ready to receive her."

At their evening devotions there was a special prayer for the widow and the destitute, and fervent thanksgiving for the many mercies bestowed upon that humble household, for the comforts of this life and the richer blessing of faith in Christ, and a hope of future blessedness in a life that shall know no end, where there will be no sin, sickness, nor sorrow.

Early the next morning Clarence went to tell Sandy, the gardener, of his intended journey to the city. Various were the commissions for seeds and plants which Clarence was to execute in the city, at Sandy's request.

" Take good care of your money," said Sandy, as he gave him ten dollars for the purchases; " there are lots of thieves about that big town, and a lad like you must look sharp about him."

" Thank you. I shall be on my guard. I had my pocket picked once upon a time," said Clarence, laughing, as he remembered his journey to " cool."

" Have you heard from the young master lately? " asked Sandy.

" Not for a month past," was the reply. " When I heard from Mr. Amadore last, he was on his way to Switzerland."

Harvey was travelling in Europe with a tutor, and was not expected home for a year or two.

Clarence bade " good morning" to Sandy, and, with carpet-bag in hand, walked two miles and a half to the nearest railroad station.

CHAPTER XXIV.

CLARENCE IN A QUANDARY.

It was evening when Clarence arrived in New York. He went directly to the —— Hotel, and inquired for Mrs. Rose. He was told that no such person was there. Much puzzled to know what to do next, he at length remembered that it was a month since she arrived in New York. Then he asked the clerk at the office to look at the register, and see if Mrs. Rose's name were not on the book at that date.

" I should remember it if there had been such a person. I haven't time to hunt over the book. Go away, boy; I must attend to this gentleman. Your name, if you please, sir," said the clerk, to a gentleman in black, who stood by the side of Clarence.

" Rev. Albertus Warren, Raceville," was the reply.

Clarence started and exclaimed, " Mr. Warren! Is it possible! Don't you know me?"

" Can it be Clarence Rose? Why, you have grown a foot taller and many inches broader than when we parted, and you don't lisp at all. I am glad to see you. For whom were you inquiring?"

" For Mrs. Rose," replied Clarence, his eyes filling with tears.

" No. 49, sir," said the clerk. " Will you have your trunk taken to your room?"

" Not just this moment. I think you refused to look for the name of Mrs. Rose on your register. Please do so at once. What was the date, Clarence?"

" About the last of November."

" Only Mrs. Rose? Not Mr. Rose?"

" Mrs. Rose, alone," was the sorrowful reply. " Mr. Rose is dead."

After a few moments' search the clerk found the name on the register — "Mrs. Rose, from California; staid three days."

" And where did she go then?"

" Don't know," was the curt reply.

" Where are you going to-night, Clarence?" asked Mr. Warren, kindly.

" I have formed no plan for the night. I suppose I can stay here."

" Very well. Give me a room with two beds," said Mr. Warren to the clerk, " and take my trunk and this young gentleman's carpet-bag to my room, and put his name on the register — Clarence Rose."

The supercilious clerk gave an almost audible sneer as he looked at the plain, homely garb, and the old, worn carpet-bag of the " young gentleman," and said, " Well, then, No. 14."

Clarence, however plainly dressed, was more neat and tidy than many a boy with richer clothing. He followed Mr. Warren to the room with "two beds," most thankful to have met with so kind a friend.

"After supper we will have a long talk, Clarence," said Mr. Warren. "You look fatigued, though, I should judge, in excellent health. Let me see; it must be two years and more since we parted. Come, let us go to supper now."

After supper the travellers returned to No. 14, and Clarence had a long story to tell, to which Mr. Warren listened with great interest.

"We are both fatigued, and can make no further inquiry for Mrs. Rose to-night."

"How did you cure yourself of the defect in your speech? You used to lisp badly," said Mr. Warren.

"My good sister Lucy took great pains with me, and with a mighty effort I succeeded in keeping my tongue behind my teeth when I said the letter S; and," added Clarence, laughing, "Harvey gave me a cow as a reward for my successful effort."

"Harvey is a noble boy; one of the best I have ever known. He will become, I trust, an excellent man, an honor to his country and a blessing to the world. I am sorry that I shall have to leave you early to-morrow morning, as I am on my way to Washington on urgent business."

The next morning, very early, Mr. Warren awakened Clarence, and told him he was just about to leave; and, said he, "I advise you, Clarence, to go home at once; there is no probability of your finding Mrs. Rose in this great city, without any clew to her whereabouts. It is expensive to be here."

"I have money enough of my own to pay my expenses," replied Clarence, proudly.

"I am glad to know it. God bless you, my boy. When you are at home again, after a while write to me. I shall be very glad to hear from you, and so will Mrs. Warren. She is much attached to you."

So saying, Mr. Warren shook hands cordially with Clarence, and hurried away.

No more sleep for Clarence that morning. He lay for a full hour meditating on what plan he should pursue to find Mrs. Rose, but was no more decided at the end of the hour than at the beginning. Yet, with the hopefulness of boyhood, he was sure "something would turn up" in his favor. So he dressed himself in his butternut brown suit, and went down to breakfast, feeling a little shy among the crowd in the large dining-room as he walked the length of it to find a place.

A waiter, who had not seen him the evening previous, addressed him sharply as he moved towards an unoccupied table.

"Boy, haven't you mistaken your place? This is the *gentlemen's* dining-room."

"I know that as well as you do," said Clarence, with perfect assurance. Taking a seat at the table,

11

he said, very decidedly and promptly, "Hand me a bill of fare."

The waiter obeyed without further questioning. Then, wondering at the sudden change in the manner of the boy, from shyness to proud assurance, he attended to him respectfully. It seemed as if the very atmosphere of the city had brought back the quondam Clarence Rose.

After breakfast, Clarence thought, as there was no probability of finding Mrs. Rose, he might as well spend the day in amusing himself, as by going directly home.

As he was passing a fashionable hatter's in Broadway, he saw some very attractive looking hats. He wore an old blue cloth cap. The temptation was too great to be resisted — at least so thought Clarence ; and after trying on a number, he at length suited himself with an expensive one, and, setting it jauntily on his head, paid for it. As he was walking out of the shop, the man of whom he had made the purchase said, —

"Young mister, here's your cap."

"I don't want it. Give it to the first beggar that comes along," replied Clarence, with an air of superlative contempt for the old friend, the blue cloth friend, who had sheltered his pate for many a month.

His next stopping-place was at Barnum's Museum, where he passed a couple of hours very much to his satisfaction.

On his way back to the —— Hotel, he stepped into a restaurant and called for a variety of nice things. When he had fully satisfied himself with them, he put his hand in his pocket for his purse — the same red silk purse that Mrs. Rose had given him when he went to school. He had had very little use for it since.

The purse was not in that pocket, neither was it in any other of his pockets. ·

While he was making this search, he was closely scrutinized by a lady and her daughter, a girl of about sixteen years, who were seated at a table very near him.

" Mother, I am sure that is little Wainbow, as we used to call him," said the daughter.

" It can't be possible; he looks more like a cloud than a rainbow in that rough overcoat."

" Rough overcoats are fashionable, mother. I am sure it is Clarence Rose : his hair is darker, and so is his complexion; but the eyes and mouth are the same. Do speak to him; pray, do. He seems in trouble."

The two ladies rose and approached Clarence. The elder said, —

" Are you Clarence Rose ? "

" I am," was the curt reply, as Clarence rose from his seat.

" I thought you were in California with your father and mother. When did you come in town ? "

"Last evening."

"Where are you staying?"

"At the —— Hotel."

"You seem to be in trouble."

"I am. While at Barnum's Museum I must have had my pocket picked, for I have lost my purse."

"You do not appear to recognize us," said the younger lady.

"I beg pardon. I was so embarrassed by the loss of my purse that I did not at first notice that it was Mrs. Snett and Miss Caroline who were speaking to me."

"Don't you remember the party at our house just before you left town to go to school?" said Miss Caroline.

"Perfectly," replied Clarence, still hunting for his purse.

"Allow me to lend you what money you need here; for I suppose you feel quite like a stranger in town after so long an absence."

"Indeed, I do," replied Clarence, his eyes moistening, and his voice faltering, in spite of a violent effort for self-control.

"Will you take a dollar, or more, if you like?"

"A dollar, if you please; where shall I return it?"

"O, we are still in Waverley Place, in the same house as when you last visited us," said Mrs.

Snett, handing him a two-dollar note. ". Tell your mother I shall soon call to see her. Good morning."

" Good morning, Clarence. I hope we shall see you again very soon," added the daughter.

" Thank you, Miss Caroline. Good morning."

As soon as the ladies left, Clarence stepped to the paying-desk, with the little round tickets left on the table for him, proving that he had spent in gratifying his palate one dollar and twenty-five cents.

He paid it as though he had indeed just returned from California, a millionnaire.

And now for the hotel. What could he do there?

He had allowed Mrs. Snett to believe that Mrs. Rose was with him at the hotel. He had told no direct falsehood, yet he had practised deception ; and what would be the consequence he could not imagine. In spite of his fashionable hat, he walked up Broadway with a gloomy, disconsolate air. He was not as manly as he thought he was while working in the garden on Linden Hill.

What he should do at the hotel he could not conceive ; but go there he must. He would go to his room No. 14, and consider.

No sooner had he entered the clerk's office than he was met by that *dignitary*, who accosted him with a supercilious air.

" Boy, you can't go to No. 14; that room is

occupied. The Rev. Mr. Warren paid your bill this morning, and said you would leave to-day."

" Very well ; so I shall," replied Clarence, greatly relieved by the generous thoughtfulness of Mr. Warren.

" Porter, bring the boy's carpet-bag," said the clerk.

Clarence took the bag, tossed the porter a quarter of a dollar, and walked off, carrying himself as stiff and erect as a raw soldier on drill.

His enemy, Pride, had not been rooted out.

Now, what was he to do in the city, with half a dollar in his pocket and a long distance from home, besides being in debt to Mrs. Snett?

" She was kind to me ; I will confess to her all the truth, and she may assist me in finding mamma."

With this thought in his mind, he walked rapidly to Waverley Place. It was now about four o'clock. As he passed from Broadway through that Place, looking for the house of Mrs. Snett, he saw the name of Hosea Fenton on a door, and instantly stopped before it. A sudden impulse seized him. He sprang up the steps and rang the bell. A waiter appeared.

" Is Mr. Fenton at home?"

" Yes, sir ; please walk into the vestibule. Your name, sir?"

" Clarence Rose."

A moment was given for reflection, and Clarence resolved to be as frank and unreserved with Mr. Fenton as he had decided to be with Mrs. Snett.

The waiter returned, and asked Clarence to lay aside his hat and overcoat.

He did so, and was shown into a large dining-room, where Mr. Fenton was seated at table alone. The first course had just been placed upon the table. Mr. Fenton was a small, gray-haired old man, dressed in a suit of snuff-colored cloth — coat, vest, and pants.

" Take a seat, Rose. Will you have soup? "

" Thank you. Yes, sir."

An extra plate had already been placed for him, and a chair beside the table, as though he had been an expected guest.

The soup was soon discussed, without a spoken word.

The second course followed.

" Fish? " said Mr. Fenton.

" Yes, sir."

" Soy? "

" No, sir."

Not another word till the fish was removed and a surloin of roast beef placed before Mr. Fenton.

" Rare or well done? "

" Well done, if you please, sir."

A custard pudding and an apple-pie followed.

" Pudding or pie? "

" Pudding, if you please, sir."

" Just as you please."

" Pudding, then."

Dried fruits and nuts followed.

"Bring the fruit and nuts to my library," said Mr. Fenton to the waiter. " Come, Rose."

Clarence followed Mr. Fenton to the library. The library was filled on all sides but one with books, and was lighted from above. At the end not occupied by bookcases was a large oil painting representing Shakespeare's Shylock and Antonio, surrounded by pictures and engravings of smaller size. A table, covered with green cloth, was in the centre of the room; a bright fire glowed in the grate. The waiter placed upon the table a tray with the fruits and nuts, and then left the room.

" Be seated, Rose," said Mr. Fenton, seating himself by the table in a large arm-chair, covered with green morocco, and pointing to one opposite to them of the same kind.

Clarence sunk into its luxurious embrace.

Mr. Fenton regarded him curiously with his keen dark eyes for full two minutes, and then said, " Nuts, nuts; help yourself."

The keen inspection daunted and embarrassed Clarence, and much as he liked nuts and dried fruit, he had now no inclination for them.

" Keep me company, Rose," said the old man, taking a few almonds.

" Thank you ; " and Clarence did the same.

" Now, tell me what brings you to town."

" I have a long story to tell, if you will have the kindness to listen to it."

" Nothing better to do for the next hour ; but be as brief as possible."

Clarence then told of the death of Mr. Rose ; the return of Mrs. Rose, and her condition, "poor and sick ; " his coming to New York ; and what had since happened to the time of his seeing the name of Hosea Fenton upon the door, and his sudden impulse to ring the bell.

" Well, what do you think induced that impulse ? "

" It probably was a remembrance of the excellent advice you gave me, sir, through Harvey Amadore."

" Have you profited by that advice ? "

" Not much, I fear ; I flattered myself I had, before I came to the city ; but I find I am the same being still, full of faults, and very weak and silly."

" What were you intending to do next ? "

" To go directly home, if I could borrow the money for that purpose," replied Clarence, a bright color spreading over his whole face.

" What ?   Without finding Mrs. Rose ! "

" I don't know how to find her."

" Have you tried ? "

"Only by asking at the hotel."

"Set to work again, and see if you can't discover some other way. When you went to school, I suppose you wrote in your copy-book, '*Perseverantia vincit omnia.*'"

"If I only knew how and where to begin."

"Harvey has given me, from time to time, a good account of you, and of all your family; and though I had never seen you, I had, for his sake as well as your own, taken an interest in you. Your frankness has pleased me. It is getting too late for you to do anything further this evening; so you must make yourself contented here, and think the matter over while I am absent."

Taking out his watch, Mr. Fenton started up, saying, "The hour is up; I must be off; but here are some letters from Harvey for your amusement; but don't forget that you are to think out some plan for finding poor Mrs. Rose. Make yourself at home."

Harvey's letters interested Clarence exceedingly. He had first travelled through England and Scotland, and was now on the continent. Several times Clarence was mentioned. Once he says, "I should like to hear of the welfare of the Paverley family. I wrote to Clarence from Edinburgh, but have not received an answer. I am anxious about Clarence." In another letter, he writes, "Still I hear nothing from Clarence. I think he has my banker's address." Again he writes, " I am anxious about Clarence. I fear he is not doing well, and is discontented with his present employment. Would it be advisable to find some other that would suit him better? I know, my dear guardian, that you strongly and persistently advised me not to separate him from his family. As for Peter, he will do very well where he is, and, no doubt, make an excellent farmer; and I should not be surprised if he became a much stronger man every way than his brother. Poor Clarence was so petted and coddled in early life as to become enervated, and incapable, I fear, of doing much for himself, or for others. However, when I left home, I had confidence in him, and hoped that he was doing well. I am much attached to him, and should be sadly disappointed if he became un-worthy of respect and affection."

Clarence was half pleased and half provoked by this notice of himself. Harvey's continued interest, when surrounded by scenes so new and attractive, surprised and gratified him; but then the doubts expressed annoyed and vexed him.

" I will disappoint Harvey," he thought to him-self; " I will be all and more than he expects."

With this resolution on his mind, he set himself to considering what he should do to find Mrs. Rose.

While thus employed the waiter lighted the gas in the library.

Soon after Mr. Fenton returned home, and found Clarence in the library, with his arms resting upon the table, and his head dropped upon them.

Mr. Fenton smiled significantly, for he thought the boy was fast asleep.

But no; Clarence surprised him by lifting his head suddenly, and exclaiming, "I have it; — I have it!"

So deeply was he absorbed in thought that he had not noticed the entrance of Mr. Fenton.

"You have it. Well, we will have tea."

So saying Mr. Fenton rang the bell, and gave orders to have the tea-equipage brought to the library.

"You see how I live alone, and have my own bachelor ways," said he, seating himself by the table.

Mr. Hosea Fenton was a banker, — a man good on 'Change for a million, — a man whose honesty and sterling integrity were proverbial.

Tea and toast were brought in.

"What are you going to do with yourself this evening?" demanded Mr. Fenton.

"Inquire about Mrs. Rose; I have thought of a plan to find where she is."

"Put that off till morning; after tea go in to see my neighbor, Mrs. Snett."

Clarence started, blushed, and stammered out at last, "But I owe her two dollars; and worse than that, I deceived her about mamma."

" But what if, in consequence of that deception, she should call at the hotel to-morrow, and find there that you had deceived her? Better go and tell her the whole truth, as you told it to me."

" But she may have company, and I am not fit to appear among genteel people."

" Genteel ! " exclaimed Mr. Fenton, with a contemptuous pursing up of the mouth. " Pshaw! don't talk to me about genteel people. I despise that word. Why are you not fit to see an old acquaintance? "

." My dress I mean, sir."

" Your dress ! Why, it is as good as mine, and nearly the same color; perhaps not quite as fine a cloth. Old Thomas Fuller, a quaint old writer, says, ' Why should any brag of what's but borrowed? Should the ostrich snatch off the gallant's feather, the beaver his hat, the goat his gloves, the sheep his coat, the silkworm his stockings, the calf his shoes, he would be left in a cold condition.' How much money had you in your purse when your pocket was picked? "

"Twenty dollars of my own, and ten that Sandy, the head gardener, gave me, with which I was to buy seeds, and some other things."

Twenty dollars Clarence had earned literally "in the sweat of his brow."

Mr. Fenton took from a large pocket-book notes to the amount of thirty dollars, and handed them to

Clarence, saying, gravely, " I do not give you this money ; it belongs to Harvey Amadore ; I lend it to you, and expect you to pay him the full amount."

" Gladly will I do that," said Clarence, eagerly, seizing the money, and thrusting it into his vest pocket.

" So that is the way you are going to carry your money, youngster ; after having been robbed, too?"

" I have no purse, sir."

" True ; take my wallet ; it has been a lucky one ; " and Mr. Fenton handed Clarence an old leather wallet that had served its wealthy owner for at least twenty years. " Now, take special care of it, and remember, when you use it, that for every dollar you put into it you are accountable for a right use, not to me, but to the Giver of every good gift. Now you can go in to see Mrs. Snett ; she lives at the next house but one from mine."

" But allow me to tell you of a way I have thought of to find out about Mrs. Rose."

" Certainly."

" I will inquire of the porter at the —— Hotel if he carried trunks for a lady, at such a date, the day when she left the hotel, and where he carried them ; or I can inquire of the drivers of the —— Hotel carriages. It is possible that some one may remember having left Mrs. Rose at the place where she now is."

" Very well, Clarence ; I am glad you have

thought out an expedient, and hope it may prove successful. When you return from Mrs. Snett's, the waiter will show you directly to your room. Good night."

"Good night, and many thanks for your kindness. Can I go to the room you are so kind as to offer me for the night? I wish to put myself a little in order before going to see Mrs. Snett."

"Well, I suppose soap and water, brush and comb, will do you no harm," said Mr. Fenton, facetiously, as he rang a bell for the waiter.

CHAPTER XXV.

A CONFESSION.

IT cost Clarence a mighty effort to summon resolution to tell Mrs. Snett the story of Mrs. Rose's misfortunes and the change in his own circumstances ; and still more, to confess the deception he had practised upon her at the restaurant. As he stood upon the door-step, he twice laid his hand upon the bell-knob, and withdrew it. He was sorely tempted to go directly out of town. But better thoughts prevailed, and, with a sudden impulse, he gave the bell a tremendous pull, startling the whole household, as a policeman might have done had the house been on fire.

The waitress, who came to the door, cautiously opened it just far enough to see, by the light of the street-lamp, an inoffensive-looking, tall boy, who asked for Mrs. Snett, and wished to see her alone.

"What name shall I give?"

"I haven't a card with me. Tell Mrs. Snett it is Clarence Rose."

"Yes;" and the door was closed in his face.

Soon the waitress returned, and showed Clarence up stairs into Mrs. Snett's dressing-room, saying there was company in the parlors, and Mrs. Snett would see him there.

Somewhat alarmed at the summons, Mrs. Snett made her appearance. She was in full dress, looking, Clarence thought, exactly as she did at the party in that same house where he had made himself so conspicuous by his dress and manners.

"Good evening, Clarence; I hope you do not bring any bad news from your mamma."

"I wish I could bring any news whatever from her, for I don't know where to find her."

"Goodness! Is she lost?" exclaimed the good lady. "I thought something dreadful was coming, from your frightened expression. Why, you are as pale as death. Tell me at once, what is it that so alarms you?"

"Have you time to hear a long story, and a sad one?"

"I can be spared from the young folks below for

a short time. Do make haste, however, for my curiosity is at the highest pitch."

Clarence now, as briefly as possible, told of his being obliged to leave school and go to his own mother, when Mrs. Snett interrupted him : —

"What, is it possible ! Wasn't Mrs. Rose your own mother?"

"No; my own mother is a poor woman, and Mrs. Rose adopted me when I was very young."

Clarence then went on, and told how he went home, with the expectation of going back to live with Mr. and Mrs. Rose, when they returned from California. Then he told of the long sickness and death of Mr. Rose, and the destitute condition of Mrs. Rose; her return to New York, and his want of success in search of her; the robbery at the Museum; and the deception he had, without any previous intention, practised upon Mrs. Snett at the restaurant. Then he mentioned that he had been very kindly received by Mr. Hosea Fenton, who had loaned him money, — which, of course, he should repay as soon as he had earned it.

Here Clarence handed a two-dollar note to Mrs. Snett.

"No, no; keep it, I entreat you. Is it possible that you are the same Clarence Rose that the children called little Wainbow? You, who lisped in such a silly way, — excuse me, — and cared for

12

nothing but a fine dress. You are wonderfully changed for the better."

"Thank you," said Clarence, with a smile. "Thank you; but please take the money. Indeed, you would oblige me by taking it."

"If you insist, I must;" and Mrs. Snett reluctantly took it, saying, "Your mamma was a friend of mine, a true friend, when I was myself in trouble, and I have not forgotten it. What can I do to aid you?"

"I am afraid there is no way in which you can help me to find out where she is."

"Yes, there is! there is!" exclaimed Mrs. Snett, with extreme animation. "Do you remember old Biddy, your mamma's cook?"

"To be sure I do — a faithful creature."

"Well, she has been here several times, since Mrs. Rose went to California, to know if I had heard from her former mistress. She said she was no longer able to go out to service, but maintained herself by clear-starching and goffering — doing up laces and fine muslins for ladies. I engaged her to do the same for me. I took her address, and have several times sent my breakfast-caps to her. Only last week she came, saying she had a sick friend with her. Biddy seemed in trouble. And besides giving her work to do for me, I asked if she would take some jelly to her sick friend. The poor creature was delighted; tears were actually in her poor old eyes. Now, I suspect Mrs. Rose is the sick friend. I will give you Biddy's address, or I will go with you myself to-morrow."

" I should be much obliged to you for the address ; and if you will excuse me, I would rather go first by myself."

Here the waitress came with a request from Miss Caroline that Mrs. Snett would not keep *Mr. Rose* any longer to herself, but " would she please come down to the parlor with Mr. Rose ? "

Clarence started up, and begged to be excused. Mrs. Snett entreated him in vain to join the young people ; but he persisted in his refusal. She then gave him the address, and begged him to let her know the result of his inquiries as soon as possible.

Clarence left the house with a heart much lighter than it was when he pulled the door-bell so violently, though it did throb somewhat as he perceived two or three young girls slyly watching his retreat as he passed through the hall, and imagined they might be some of his former companions.

For the first time since Clarence left his home he remembered his mother's injunction, " not to forget his prayers ; " and in the quietness of the large room appropriated to his use, he knelt by the bedside, penitent for sins and errors, thankful for the protection and guidance of his heavenly Father, and begging to be aided in the search for the friend whom he truly loved.

CHAPTER XXVI.

BIDDY MEGAN.

" Tenth Avenue, number —, fifth floor. Mrs. Megan."

This was the address given to Clarence by Mrs. Snett.

Early the next morning he stood before a huge, ugly tenement-house, where rags and old hats were abundant, judging by the sham panes protruding from the windows. And he must mount to the fifth floor of that house, crammed as it was, from attic to basement, with miserable specimens of humanity. The staircase was absolutely filthy; and poor Clarence, with whom " neatness was next to the cardinal virtues," picked his way daintily up the four flights of stairs, shoving aside here and there a white, or rather blue-headed child, who eagerly shrieked, " Give me a penny; give me a penny."

At last he found the door on the right, at the back of the house, and knocked there.

Mrs. Megan, the veritable Biddy, lifted the latch with her elbow, and appeared with her hands wearing white gloves — of starch. Those hands were now lifted with amazement at the sight of Clarence, and then, with what might be termed an Irish howl, were laid upon his shoulders.

"Who is it? Who is it?" came from a feeble voice in one corner of the small room.

"Your own swate darlint," was the reply, with a brogue too rich for any tongue but a Hibernian to describe or to imitate.

Clarence stepped forward, and there, indeed, was Mrs. Rose, pale and sick; the hair, that had been black as the raven's wing, now almost white, and her features as pinched and thin as if she had been starved in a southern prison.

"Mamma!" It was the only word Clarence could utter, and then he was forced to give way to a complete deluge of tears.

"*My* Clarence! So, you have not forsaken me!"

"No, indeed!" replied Clarence, partially recovering himself, and pressing one of those thin white hands to his lips as he stood by the bedside; "no, indeed! how could I forsake you!"

Meanwhile, Biddy was disposing of her *gloves* in a basin of water, and then with a towel wiping the prints from the shoulders of Clarence — a circumstance which quite changed the pathos of the scene into the ludicrous — which, however, did not at the time strike the principal actors in the scene.

"I have come to take you home with me, mamma."

"Home! I have no home."

"But I have," said Clarence, with emphasis, looking round the miserable apartment, and contrasting it with the neat little parlor prepared for the reception of Mrs. Rose.

"Sit ye down," said Biddy, handing her only chair, and then discreetly leaving the room.

"I only received your letter three days since, and started immediately for New York. I could learn nothing of you at the —— Hotel; but I met Mrs. Snett, and she told me where I might possibly find you."

"Mrs. Snett! She was once a good friend of mine; but I suppose, like all the rest, she would not acknowledge my acquaintance now."

"You are mistaken, mamma; she wants to come and see you, and speaks of you gratefully and affectionately. Why did you not go to her, or let her know you were in town?"

"Because I sent to two ladies with whom I was formerly acquainted, and they took not the least notice of me. I thought they were all alike. Then I sent for Biddy; she, dear, good soul, took me in, and has nursed me and cared for me as she would have done for an infant. I charged her not to name me to any person whatever, as I should not live long; and when money was needed to bury me, she could dispose of the remainder of my wardrobe, and that would be sufficient to pay all expenses."

"O, mamma, don't talk so dolefully; the country

air will do you good, and my mother and sister will
be so kind to you! They are grateful to you, —
don't look doubtful, — they are, indeed, and will do
everything in their power for your comfort."

" Can it be? I have thought of nothing lately but
being prepared for death ; and there was nothing in .
my former life to give me the least consolation in view
of that solemn hour — I could only throw myself
upon the mercy of God. O, I am afraid of death."

" But I cannot spare you yet, mamma. Cheer
up, and prepare to go home with me."

" That does not seem possible. And yet, I
ought not to be a burden to poor Biddy. Look at
that stove. All day long, when she is not caring
for me, she is washing, starching, and ironing."

" And almost suffocating you with the heat and
smoke."

" They do affect my breathing, it is true, and
take away my appetite."

" To-morrow, then, we will leave."

" How can I leave my good Biddy? "

Clarence thought a moment, and then said, —

" We can take her with us. Here she comes. I
will tell her all about the plan, in the entry. Come,
Biddy, I want to have a consultation with you."

" Was there iver the bate of this! Why, my
lady, the boy is a man," exclaimed Biddy; " he
don't talk any more like a babby."

A long consultation was holden in the entry, and

Biddy finally consented to go to Hodgton, and have everything ready in two days, or three, for their departure. When Clarence returned to the room, Mrs. Rose said, —

"Indeed, Clarence, Biddy is right; you have gotten the entire use of your tongue. You no longer twist and wriggle it as you used to. I already feel better, much better, for seeing you, and knowing that you have not forgotten and forsaken me. Good by, for a while, dearest; but come in again to-morrow."

"Certainly. And may I bring Mrs. Snett with me?"

"No, Clarence. I may be pardoned for a little lingering pride. I would not willingly see Mrs. Snett in this miserable place."

"No, indade. I never let on to anybody that my mistress was in such a place as this," said poor old Biddy.

"A place but too good for me, Biddy, dear," said Mrs. Rose, with the first tears that she had shed during this interview.

Clarence hastened back to Mr. Fenton, to tell him of the result of his search. That gentleman had gone to his banking-house, and would not be home till dinner-time.

Clarence then went to Mrs. Snett, to tell her of his success, and to thank her for putting him in the way of it. He softened as much as possible Mrs.

Rose's refusal to see Mrs. Snett, by telling her it really was not a fit place for any lady, and hardly safe, as the air was excessively disagreeable.

" But I must see her. I shall go and bring her here, till she is ready to go home with you. I will not take a refusal.".

Clarence could no further oppose this good lady, but only requested that she would wait till the next day. Then he went back to Mr. Fenton's, and, in the library, wrote a long letter to his mother and sister.

———————◆———————

CHAPTER XXVII.

THE BANKER'S HOME.

CLARENCE had just finished his letter when he was summoned to dinner.

The conversation at table was as brief between Mr. Fenton and his visitor as it had been the previous day. But when the nuts and fruit were in the library, and they were seated at the green table, Mr. Fenton said, " Now, boy, give me an account of your morning's doings."

Clarence did so, giving the particulars very clearly and candidly.

" I know now why Harvey Amadore has formed so strong an attachment to you, in spite of your many faults of character," remarked Mr. Fenton, giving Clarence one of those peculiarly penetrative glances, which were rather embarrassing.

Clarence cracked a nut, and made no reply.

"You are grateful; now, true gratitude is an attribute of noble minds. Mrs. Rose petted and almost spoiled you; and, instead of resenting it, you wish to do everything in your power for her."

"O, sir — do not blame her; she was exceedingly kind to me; and if it were mistaken indulgence, still it was meant for kindness."

"That's right, boy; stand up for her. I like that spirit, especially when a friend is poor and in trouble. But how do you expect to maintain this woman, after you have taken her home?"

"We have more than enough for ourselves, all united as we are as a family; and we shall be right glad to make Mrs. Rose comfortable in our cottage. O, sir, if you had seen her in that horrid dirty house, you would not wonder at my being in a hurry to get her out of it."

"You said the twenty dollars you lost had been laid aside from your earnings; what did you expect to do with it?"

Clarence hesitated a moment, his face red as a peony, and then he replied, frankly, "I intended to buy myself some nicer clothing; but I can do very well without it."

"So you can; but now, answer another question

as candidly as you did the last. What business or profession are you looking forward to in the future?"

"Sir, I am a gardener, and I expect to be a gardener. I like the employment."

"Right! Capitally right! If God, in his wise providence, calls you from a garden to a seat in the Senate of the United States, you will be prepared for it, as the shepherd David was to be king over Israel; but never look forward to it as an end.

> 'Act, act in the living present;
> Heart within, and God o'erhead.'

"This reminds me," continued Mr. Fenton, "of an anecdote told by my favorite old writer, Thomas Fuller. It seems a farmer, who was a relation of the Bishop of Lincoln, asked the bishop to bestow an office upon him. 'Cousin,' quoth the bishop, 'if your cart be broken, I'll mend it; if your plough is old, I'll give you a new one, and seed to sow your land; but a husbandman I found you, and a husbandman I leave you.'"

"My brother is a farmer," said Clarence; "but my employment is among flowers and shrubs, and where I enjoy the beautiful. O, sir, I wish you could see our green-house! Our camellias are splendid, and our azaleas magnificent. Next spring do come and see our rhododendrons."

Mr. Fenton smiled, and nodded his head approvingly at this burst of enthusiasm.

"Sandy, the head gardener, is the wisest, shrewdest old Scotchman! You ought to hear him quote from his favorite Burns. Why, he knows all Burns's poems by heart. I think Sandy is one of the happiest men in the world."

Mr. Fenton sighed deeply.

"I hope, sir, I have not displeased you," said Clarence, anxiously.

"No, no, boy; I was only thinking how much more real, rational enjoyment there must be in cultivating beautiful flowers and fruits, in the pure country air, than in the harassing accumulation of wealth, shut up within the brick walls of a banker's office. Well has the poet Cowper said, 'God made the country, but man made the town.' I was myself a farmer's boy, in beautiful Orange County; there I passed the happiest years of my life. There, too, I fitted for college; but thirst for gold brought me to the city, and here I have moiled and toiled till I can count my hundreds of thousands of solid coin; but alas! how much solid pleasure I have lost!"

CHAPTER XXVIII.

SIGHT-SEEING.

THE following morning the weather was rainy, and Mr. Fenton at the breakfast-table said to Clarence that there was going to be a long storm.

"Then I am afraid mamma will not be able to take a journey for some time yet," replied Clarence, with a troubled expression.

"Make yourself easy; your azaleas and camellias will not miss you, and I should; for I am becoming quite fond of your company."

"Thank you, sir; I was afraid you would be quite tired of me by this time. I shall go to see mamma, and I am sure Mrs. Snett will not venture out in the storm."

"And now you have an opportunity, you had better see some of the city sights besides Barnum's," said Mr. Fenton, with a merry twinkling of his dark eyes and a quirk of the mouth. "Here," he continued, "is a ticket to a fine horticultural exhibition; and here is another that will admit you to the rooms of the Historical Society. I hope you will have a profitable day; and mind, leave your money at home, so that pickpockets can have no chance, nor the shopkeepers either."

Clarence could not help smiling, though he felt ashamed of himself, and replied, "You are too good to me, sir; I have not deserved so much kindness."

"We all get more than we deserve from our heavenly Father; and if he gives us an opportunity to show kindness to others, we ought to be thankful for it. Good morning."

Clarence, thinking so early a visit might not be welcome to Mrs. Rose, went first to the horticultural exhibition, and passed there a charming hour, delighted with the splendid display of flowers and hot-house fruits.

When he reached Ninth Avenue, and came near to the tenement-house where he had found Mrs. Rose, he saw a carriage standing before the door. Mrs. Snett had come, in spite of the rain, to see her quondam friend, Mrs. Rose.

As Clarence drew near, Biddy rushed from the house with an old umbrella over her head, and stood by the carriage door, the glass of which was down.

"No, indade, my good lady; my mistress will not let you come up them nasty stairs. She thanks you for coming, a thousand, thousand times. She is better to-day for seeing the swate young master yesterday; and sure, here he is!"

"I am sorry, very sorry Mrs. Rose cannot see me, Clarence; give my kindest regards to her, and beg her to come to me, and stay with me till she is well enough to take the journey."

"I will do so; but I fear she will not consent," said Clarence.

"You make a mistake, Master Clarence; if mistress is as well to-morrow as she is to-day, and the good lady will send her coach, I will carry mistress down stairs and put her in myself; then I can have a chance to be all ready to go to the counthry wid ye."

"Come close, Biddy," said Mrs. Snett, handing out a basket to her, and adding, "I will call for Mrs. Rose to-morrow at eleven o'clock. Good morning, Clarence; give my best love to your mamma."

Then ordering the coachman to drive home, the carriage was soon out of sight.

"I am sorry mamma would not see Mrs. Snett," said Clarence, as he ascended the staircase, followed by Biddy, with the basket on her arm.

"Indade, and indade, it was all me own doing; I wouldn't have the lady see my mistress in such a 'bominable room for all the gould in Californy."

"Then you took it upon yourself to refuse?"

"Sure, I did; don't you think I've got some pride for the family I've sarved a dozen years? Biddy knows what she's about."

By this time they had reached the "'bominable room."

Mrs. Rose was sitting up in the one chair, an old wooden one, dressed in a rich but faded blue silk, with a red Cashmere shawl — a real Cashmere — wrapped about her, and a pair of silk shoes upon her small feet. The beloved Cashmere was the only article of great value she had retained, and that she had clung to desperately, having made it, as many do, quite an idol.

Clarence was struck with the painful contrast between her dress and the surroundings. It was pitiful indeed; but he said, cheerily, " I am right glad to see you better to-day, mamma; I hope you will soon be quite well again."

" This is the first time I have been dressed since I left that horrid hotel. Biddy was so anxious to see me sitting up, that I have made the effort, and I feel really better for it."

Biddy now came forward with a board on which she was accustomed to iron, and on the board was now placed what she called a " lunchy."

This consisted of sandwiches, wine jelly, and ice-cream, in beautiful china and glass.

With a ceremonious courtesy, Biddy presented the tray before Mrs. Rose, who looked at it with as much astonishment as if it had dropped from the skies; she, however, asked no questions; for in her weak, suffering condition, she had yielded herself entirely to Biddy's care and control.

Mrs. Rose eagerly helped herself, looking at the beautiful plate, upon which she placed a sandwich, with childish delight.

Biddy then handed the *tray* to Clarence, giving him a mischievous wink, as he took a saucer of ice-cream ; as much as to say, " We know, we know."

Clarence took the hint, and said nothing about Mrs. Snett.

" I think I shall be able to go with you, dear, when the storm is over," said Mrs. Rose, as she took a glass of jelly ; " I grow stronger every minute."

After a half hour's talk, Mrs. Rose appeared fatigued, and Clarence bade her " good morning," leaving it for Biddy to give such information as she pleased about the call of Mrs. Snett, and the arrangements for the morrow.

Much to his satisfaction, Clarence passed the hours till dinner-time at the rooms of the Historical Society, examining, with intelligent curiosity, the various contributions to nature and art.

CHAPTER XXIX.

PETE.

THE next morning, before breakfast, the postman · brought a letter to Clarence from Pete. It was addressed to " Clarence Rose Paverley, Esq., to be left at No. 14 Waverley Place, for him. City of New York."

13

Clarence had mentioned Mr. Fenton's address in his letter home. Pete wrote as follows: —

DEAR CLARENCE: Didn't you have a time, finding your mammy! I'm glad you did find her at last, and such a grand friend as Mr. Fenton; isn't he bully? Don't get too grand yourself, you know you kinder lean that way. There isn't much news to tell; we are getting along pretty much after the old way, if the spring comes on early, we shall begin to plough soon. What do you think has happened to our old speckled hen Nabby! Why she up and died, leaving her five chicks for me to bring up by hand. Three of them are yellow, and two speckled. The yellow ones I've named Rough and Ready, Fuss and Feathers, and Old Hickory, the speckled, Grace Darling, and Bunchy. Rough and Ready is a real fighter; he tries to drive away Bunchy, from the feed, I give from my hand, Indian meal and water, you know he has a special spite against Bunchy, I suppose it is because she's so ugly, like you Clarence, Rough and Ready don't like ugly things. You didn't like your old blue cap, O you would soon get back, your city notions. We've got the parlor all fixed up for your mammy, everything in apple-pie order. Mother says she don't believe, the poor lady will be able to travel, as soon as you thought, and that is the reason I write to you now, hoping you

will get this as directed. I set down as soon, as
we got your letter, and wrote; I haven't put any
date, for I haven't got the Almanac, and don't remember it. Lucy would send some message if she
knew I was writing, but she don't, nor don't mother,
'cause, I didn't want to tell her that I send you five
dollars in this, 'cause I'm afraid you won't have
money enough to get home without, If you think
you will, though, pay it to Mr. Hosea Fenton on
account, or buy some seeds for Sandy, just which
you think best. Clarence, you are a queer fellow,
I can't quite make you out, any way I can fix it.

I am your brother, to command, &c., &c.

PETER PAVERLEY.

P, S, Now I think on't, you may spend one
dollar, of my money to buy a farming-book, you
know what I mean, some good book, all about
farmers, and farming.

P, S, Number 2. I don't know how, to make
my stops, properly so I have scattered, them all the
way, through about regular, distances just as I
plant corn.

At the breakfast-table Mr. Fenton told Clarence
that the weather was too severe for Mrs. Rose to
venture out, and that Mrs. Snett ought not to go
for her.

" I advise you to step in after breakfast, and say

to that good lady, with my compliments, that I do not think it prudent for an invalid to venture out in this storm. Then go and tell Mrs. Rose so. After you have seen her, come back here and write to Harvey. Tell him candidly, and fully too, all you have told me since you have been in the city. A steamer for Havre leaves to-morrow, and I will forward your letter."

Clarence followed Mr. Fenton's advice.

To his surprise, when he mentioned this advice to Mrs. Rose, she had not heard a word from Biddy about such an arrangement as had been made the day previous.

"Clarence, dear," said Mrs. Rose, sadly, "I wouldn't go to Mrs. Snett's on any account. I have nothing fit to wear. Look at my old faded finery, and I am sure you will excuse the small remnant of pride I have left. I am truly grateful for her kindness. I cast my bread upon the waters in this instance, and it has returned to me. There is such a thing as gratitude in the world. Here are three persons who prove it — Mrs. Snett, yourself, and my kind Biddy."

"But would it not be well for you to try your strength, mamma, by going first to Mrs. Snett's if the weather should be pleasant to-morrow ; and, besides, you would then give Biddy an opportunity to attend to what preparations are necessary for moving."

" Biddy has already disposed of all her worldly possessions to a fellow-tenant," replied Mrs. Rose, with a sad smile, " and has gone out to buy me a coarse cloak for travelling. I shall be ready to go to-morrow if the weather proves favorable."

Poor Biddy to buy a cloak with her own money, and Mrs. Rose to wear a cashmere worth eight hundred dollars! What a lesson on the love of dress — the ruling passion, strong in sickness and poverty! The lesson was not lost upon Clarence.

" So you leave me to-morrow, Clarence, should the weather be favorable," said Mr. Fenton, as they were seated in the library at the usual hour in the evening.

" I do, sir."

" And you expect to be able to maintain Mrs. Rose, at your mother's."

" We are willing to do so."

" But are you able?"

" I have heard of an old proverb — ' Where there's a will there's a way ; ' and I am beginning to find the truth of it," replied Clarence, with a bright smile.

" Very well. A strong will is an excellent thing. No one can be truly manly without a strong will ; but the will must be governed by right principles and good sense. Fools are obstinate ; wise men are reasonable and open to conviction. I have become much interested in you, Clarence, and shall be sorry to part with you. It may seem strange to you that I do not assist you in a pecuniary way."

"No, indeed," interrupted Clarence, eagerly; "I have not thought of such aid, nor wished for it. I am exceedingly obliged to you for all your kindness since I have been in the city."

"And I intend to continue that interest. I shall wish to hear from you, from time to time, by letter. You must make your own way in the world. We talk about great men having been self-made. In fact there is no such thing; they are God-made. From the first there was the original character, with its faculties and tendencies; then, the influence of circumstances, the 'guinea stamp,' as your friend Sandy would say."

"But the man's the gold for all that, and all that."

"Some men become brass, others iron, and others nothing but dull lead. I hope for you, Clarence, better things. You were, for a while, placed under circumstances not favorable to a true, manly development of character; but you are overcoming those weakening influences, and, I have no doubt, with God's help you will overcome them entirely. You will, in part, be under the same influence again. Do not be misled through your kindness. You have the example of an excellent Christian mother and sister, and, if I am not mistaken, your younger brother has a strong character."

"He has, sir, a stronger character than mine; but he is as rough as a bear."

"Well, polish is not effected upon soft materials. The diamond, for example, receives polish; sandstone does not. The polish that a man needs is not the external flourish and pretension of a dandy; but an American should be a plain gentleman, — *gentle* — that is the *suaviter in modo* — *man*, the FORTITER IN RE.

"You say you are a gardener," continued Mr. Fenton; "here are some books I have purchased for you on gardening, and two on architecture; for I think in time you may be disposed to unite the two arts."

The books were beautifully bound, and illustrated with colored engravings.

"You have room for them in your carpet-bag," said Mr. Fenton, as Clarence, quite overcome with surprise, was for a moment unable to speak. He found his voice, however, and warmly thanked Mr. Fenton for the beautiful present.

"I perceive that you have taste that only needs cultivation to render you a genuine artist in your line. It is a good gift, and you will, no doubt, make a right use of it," he continued; "I haven't told you the latest news from Harvey. He intends to be home in May or June."

"Indeed! How happy we shall all be to see him! Where is he now?"

"Still in Italy. No traveller has enjoyed Rome more than our young friend. He has been studying the history of that wonderful empire in its rise and decline in the midst of its magnificent remains, and I hope he has learned many things from that history that will render him useful to his own country on his return. One thing he says he has learned by travelling more perfectly than any other."

"What is that?"

"*To prize his own country, its government and institutions, its varied climate and soil, its strong-minded men, and its virtuous, noble women.* I trust he will return prepared for a whole-souled patriot and widely-useful citizen. His boyhood has been one of rich promise."

The next morning was clear and bright; the deep-blue March sky spanning the city was almost as pure as when seen through the softened brown tracery of the budding trees of the country.

Mrs. Rose, cheered with the expectation of a change from her doleful lodgings, was in readiness for Clarence, at an early hour, to go to the station. When the carriage arrived at the door of the tenement-house (it was Mr. Fenton's handsome carriage), a crowd of squalid urchins gathered around it, and not a few heads were thrust out of the windows to see the novel sight — some in night-caps, and others with caps whose wide borders were blown back by the morning wind; others with unkempt hair streaming about their begrimed faces. Wickedness and woe dwelt there. Clarence absolutely shuddered at the shocking appearance of the front of this miserable tenement, and hurried up the long staircase. With the aid of Biddy, Clarence carried Mrs. Rose down those horrid stairs, and placed her in the vehicle which had attracted so much attention.

An express wagon had now arrived, into which Biddy placed trunks, budgets, bundles, boxes, and parcels, almost enough to fill the wagon. This was a matter of surprise to Clarence, but he asked no questions, and they drove off to the station.

No incidents worth mentioning occurred on the journey. They arrived safely, at nightfall, at the white cottage, and were cordially welcomed by the good mother and her children.

" What lots of baggage ! " exclaimed Pete, as he aided Biddy in carrying in the multitudinous and multiform articles.

Indeed, the little parlor could scarcely contain all those trunks, boxes, &c. How did Biddy ever contrive to accommodate them in her kitchen-like room at the tenement-house ! Mrs. Rose was too much fatigued to take notice of the little parlor that evening ; but the next morning, when she awoke, she looked around, and exclaimed, " Where am I ? How neat and sweet ! "

The change was indeed very delightful from that

smoky room, with its dark, dingy walls, to this bright, cheerful apartment.

Soon Lucy came in with a tray, on which was a nice breakfast, tea and toast, and a broiled young pigeon from Pete's pigeon-house.

"And you are Clarence's sister," said Mrs. Rose; "you do resemble him, strikingly. Where is Biddy? She ought to wait upon me."

"She has been, it seems, accustomed to a dairy, and was so delighted with ours that she begged to churn the butter, and let me wait upon you."

"And do you churn butter?"

"Yes, ma'am."

"You don't seem like a milkmaid at all, unless one of those fancy milkmaids of romance and poetry," said Mrs. Rose, looking admiringly at Lucy, who smiled, saying, —

"I am no fancy milkmaid or dairy-woman, but a genuine country girl, accustomed to hard work, and, formerly, to hard fare. Now we are very comfortable, and hope we shall be able to make you so."

Mrs. Rose, after breakfast, dressed herself in one of those old, faded silk gowns, and wrapped her old cashmere, that beloved cashmere, about her shoulders. She then proceeded, with Biddy's aid, to unpack her trunks and boxes.

What *lots* of old finery! Mrs. Rose had said that she was obliged to dispose of a part of her wardrobe in order to obtain money to pay her expenses home. What remained of that wardrobe was enough for three or four women of moderate requirements — laces of the most costly kind, which, Biddy said, were " as yallow as gould," and Mrs. Rose declared were all the better for that; artificial flowers enough to fit out a country milliner's show-box; ribbons of all shades and hues; satin, silk, and kid shoes; lace veils; white and black bonnets, of various fashions; and, withal, not one single, simple calico, or other dress suitable to wear among the plain, honest people at the white cottage.

When Mrs. Paverley came in, about eleven o'clock, to inquire after the health of her guest, she was astonished at the display of these articles, as they were spread out on bed, bureau, chairs, and table.

" I hope, ma'am, you are quite better this morning," said she, looking much astonished at the lady in silk and cashmere, with a lace cap, trimmed with scarlet ribbons, stuck on the back of her head.

" Thank you, Mrs. Paverley; I feel quite well; but where is Clarence? Why didn't he come in to see me this morning?"

" He has gone to his work. We breakfast at five o'clock at this season of the year, and he works in our garden for an hour before he goes to Linden Hill."

" So early! I should think it would wear him out."

"He is perfectly healthy, and, I think, is very happy, too."

"You all seem so," said Mrs. Rose, casting a look at Mrs. Paverley's homespun dress and her blue, checked apron, and then, with a sigh, turning to her own gay attire, as she thought how utterly unsuitable it was for her present circumstances.

Mrs. Paverley had no longer the sad countenance and miserable appearance with which she had presented herself at Mr. Warren's when she went for Clarence. She now looked younger than Mrs. Rose, though some years her senior.

"Where did you keep all those things in the city,—dresses, and bonnets, and shawls, and all sorts of fancy affairs?" asked Mrs. Paverley of Biddy, when she met her, after leaving Mrs. Rose.

"Why, ma'am" (we will not attempt to give the Irish brogue), "we hired a woman to keep the trunks and boxes. I was sorry to give my mistress such poor 'commodations, she who had lived so grandly. You know, she went first to a big hotel, where she had to pay three or four dollars a day,— that was too spensive; so she come to my poor lodgings. I sold some of her nice things for her, enough to pay for her board. Don't think, ma'am, she lived on poor Biddy. She wouldn't do such a thing. But then, you know, she couldn't bear to let her grand acquaintance know she was not the same great lady she was when Master Clarence lived with us. She thought, poor dear, that she was going to die, and kept a great many things, so that when she died she might have a decent burial. She wanted to be buried from Grace Church, and have as grand a funeral as any lady in the land."

Mrs. Paverley could scarcely believe Biddy's report of Mrs. Rose's intentions, and the singular pride thus evinced; doubtless allowance ought to be made for Biddy's Irish exaggeration, and her Irish notions about funerals.

CHAPTER XXX.

A VISIT TO THE GARDEN.

MARCH, with his fierce winds, had given place to weeping and smiling April; and April had yielded to her more genial sister, the English poet's darling, May; who, in turn, must yield the palm to our June — rosy, laughing June.

For the first time since her arrival at the Paverley cottage, Mrs. Rose walked to Linden Hill. It was one of those cool days in May which usually follow a rain-storm. The sky was as pure as the rose that "had been washed, just washed in a shower;" and the fresh grass reminded Mrs. Rose of a beloved

green and flowered velvet carpet, the crowning glory
of her former elegantly-furnished mansion. So she
wrapped her Cashmere about her, and picking her
way carefully, she followed the direction given her
at the cottage, and found Clarence at work in the
garden, transplanting flowers from the green-house.
He was stooping over a bed of verbenas of various
hues, when he was startled by the sound of a familiar voice : " Clarence, darling, hard at work ; you
will kill yourself. Why, you have been here ever
since six this morning, and now it is nearly four
o'clock."

" I allowed myself one hour for dinner, and another hour for reading at noon. There's no danger
of my hurting myself, Mrs. Rose ; I enjoy work.
I am obliged to do more than usual, because I am
in debt, and I am trying to get out of it. You
know I was robbed of thirty dollars in New York,
and I have had to make up that sum by extra work.
Sandy, the head gardener, has given me a piece of
ground that Mr. Amadore allowed him to use solely
for himself. Sandy has given it to me for the same
purpose, and I am raising flowers for market upon
it. I have made twenty dollars already."

" You call me Mrs. Rose, Clarence, and no longer
mamma, as you used to," said she, sadly ; " I know
I cannot do for you what I once could."

" Don't think that is the reason for the change ;
far from it. I am too old and huge a fellow now

to be calling any one mamma; it sounds babyish. But please excuse me if I go on with my work; these verbenas must all be covered from the sun, and I was going with my wheelbarrow for some flower-pots to cover them with."

So saying, Clarence trundled off the wheelbarrow, and left Mrs. Rose meditating for several minutes. While she was thus lost in thought, she was suddenly aware of the presence of a stranger, a boy, or, rather, a young man, of prepossessing appearance, apparently a couple of years older than Clarence.

He bowed politely, and passed on. Just then Clarence appeared with the wheelbarrow, loaded with the empty flower-pots.

" Is it possible ! " he exclaimed, letting the handles of the barrow drop suddenly. " Can it be Mr. Amadore ! "

" Quite possible, Clarence ; how are you?" with a cordial shake of the hand. " Have I, then, altered so much in appearance, during my absence? "

" You have indeed ; you have grown very tall, and absolutely wear a mustache. When did you arrive? "

" By the last steamer from Liverpool ; and I made my way directly home, with the exception of a few hours I passed with Mr. Fenton in New York."

" I beg your pardon, Mrs. Rose," said Clarence, as that lady stood wondering at the rencontre.

" Mr. Amadore, Mrs. Rose, the friend whom I used to call mamma when we were at school."

Mrs. Rose greeted Harvey very coolly, quite to the surprise of Clarence; and saying she was fatigued with the long walk, left the garden.

" My poor verbenas will suffer if I do not cover them," said Clarence; "I must go on with my business. Just look at them. Are they not splendid! Soon we shall have a display of rhododendrons worth looking at. I meant they should come out in all their glory in honor of your arrival; but you have taken them and me by surprise."

While Clarence was saying this he continued his work, much to the amusement of Harvey, who could scarcely realize that Clarence had become an enthusiastic " lover of flowers."

" How are Mrs. Paverley, and Miss Lucy, and Peter ? " he inquired.

" Well, thank you. Isn't that a magnificent verbena? So bright a scarlet it fairly dazzles your eyes like the sun."

" I must go and find Aunty Dotty," said Harvey. " Clarence, come to the Hall this evening; I have something to tell you from your good friend, Mr. Fenton."

" I sent him a bouquet, last week, of my choicest flowers. Did he receive it?"

" He did, and was much pleased with it." So saying, Harvey walked on, as much pleased with the enthusiasm of Clarence for his flowers, as Mr. Fenton was with the flowers themselves.

On her way back to the cottage, Mrs. Rose was grumbling to herself about Harvey Amadore. "What right has he to make a slave of Clarence ! He, an old schoolmate and professed friend ! It's too bad ! He might have done something else for him better than making him a gardener. I will give Harvey Amadore a piece of my mind, when I see him again."

With these thoughts troubling her brain and heart, she was walking slowly onward, when some one came up with her, and saluted her unceremoniously. It was Aunty Dotty.

"So you are the gay lady living on the good people at the gardener's cottage."

Mrs. Rose stared at the tall, severe-looking woman, astonished and displeased at this abrupt address.

"She's mad at me," muttered Dotty; "but I don't care a straw."

Then addressing Mrs. Rose again, "You don't know me. I am a relation of Harvey Amadore's. His father was my cousin. I have the charge of Linden Hall, and work for my living. I don't hang on to Harvey because he's a relation, or a friend. I might, if I was like some folks," she continued, with a toss of her head, and a significant glance at Mrs. Rose.

14

"Do you mean to insult me?" exclaimed Mrs. Rose, with mingled fear and anger.

"No; I mean to tell you the plain truth. You are an expense at the cottage to them Paverleys, and you do nothing but dress up fine and play grand lady. Now I should like to know how much that shawl cost that you wear so proudly."

"It is my own, and I have a right to wear it. You are very impertinent."   .

"But please tell me how much that shawl cost."

"Eight hundred dollars," blurted out Mrs. Rose, angrily.

"Eight hundred dollars! Why, the Paverleys could live on that money two whole years."

"Have they complained of my living with them?"

"Not a word of complaint, I'll venture to say, from them. They are grateful to you for taking care of the boy for so many years, though you were spoiling him with high and foolish notions."

"You are positively insulting. I wish you would leave me. You are even worse than Harvey Amadore."

"Harvey Amadore! What in the world has he done to you?"

"Nothing to me, directly; I never saw him till to-day."

"To-day! Where have you seen him to-day?"

· "Just now; in the garden at Linden Hall."

. " Goodness me ! " exclaimed Miss Dotty, turning round, and walking back to Linden Hall as fast as her feet could carry her.

CHAPTER XXXI.

SOMETHING NOT TOLD.

AFTER tea, that same evening, Clarence prepared himself to go to Linden Hall to meet Harvey.

" Now you look something as you used to," said Mrs. Rose. " Come and sit awhile in my room, before you go to see that proud Harvey Amadore."

" I have a half hour to spare," said Clarence, as they seated themselves at a window, through which the last rays of the setting sun were glinting into the room, and gorgeous clouds of purple and gold were curtaining the glowing west.

" Why do you call Harvey Amadore proud? I am sure you could have seen nothing in his manner to-day that was proud or haughty," asked Clarence.

" He was your schoolmate and friend ; why then does he place you now in a station so far below himself?"

" I am in the station in which I was born. You took me from it, Mrs. Rose, no doubt with the kindest intentions, and I am grateful to you for all your care and kindness; but it was the will of. Providence that I should return to that station. My mother is a truly excellent woman, perfectly contented with her lot; and you know what Lucy is."

" Lucy is one of a thousand," interrupted Mrs. Rose; " she would grace any station."

" And yet she has no aspirations after any other condition in life than that to which God has called her."

" Pete is just fit for a farmer, common and un-refined. I don't mind his having hard, brown hands and a freckled face, but I do grieve over the change in you, from those soft, white hands and fair complexion, to the condition in which they now are," said Mrs. Rose, with a sigh. " Couldn't you wear gloves when you are at work in the garden, if work you must?"

Clarence could not help laughing at this question. Instead of answering it, he said, —

" Pete is a noble fellow; you don't understand him. He is as faithful as yonder sun, and as honest as the man Diogenes was looking for. The philos-opher needn't have gone a step farther if he had found our Pete. He might have turned the full light of his lantern upon him without finding the least deceitfulness in word or deed."

" You are warm in your brother's defence."

" Am I? Well, he deserves it. His true man-liness has been an example to me, which I have only been able to follow at a humble distance."

" Alas! alas! Your own relations have stolen your love from your mamma." Overcome by her own morbid feelings, Mrs. Rose burst into tears.

Clarence tried to soothe her in vain. She fairly sobbed aloud. At length she restrained herself, and listened to his assurance, that he still felt the tenderest interest in her, and the greatest desire for her happiness.

A sudden thought seemed to strike her, and she said, —

" Now, Clarence, dear, if you had an opportunity to go on with your education, and to prepare yourself for one of the learned professions, would you not accept it? "

" My sentiments on this subject are well expressed in a very good book, from which I copied an extract. I have the extract in my pocket-book, or wallet, the one Mr. Fenton gave me. I like to put good things in it. May I read the extract to you? "

" If you please."

" 'It is God's will that different men should follow different pursuits, according to the station in which they were born, the gifts they possess, the circumstances in which they find themselves. Bring it down to individual cases, and the truth still holds. It is still the will of God that this man should ply a humble craft; that this other should have the duties entailed by broad acres and large property;

that a third should go to the desk and sit behind a
counter all his days; that a fourth should give his
time to the restoration of sick patients; that a fifth
should fight the battles of his country. Now, if
this is God's will in each individual case, no good,
but the greatest harm, would ensue from an individual's infringing that will; from his thrusting himself out of his own vocation into one which seems
higher and more dignified. Each man's wisdom
and happiness must consist in doing, as well as his
faculties will admit, the work which God sets him.'"

Clarence carefully folded the little paper, and replaced it in the old leather wallet.

"Now, Mrs. Rose, you see I am doing the work
to which Providence has called me. I do it because it is my duty. I do it to gain my daily bread,
and I find pleasure in it. God made flowers and
fruit beautiful and good at the creation, but he
made them, besides, capable of variety and improvement, by cultivation, to almost any extent. It is
no wonder that men have turned with disgust from
the cares and turmoil of a public and high station,
to the cultivation of even cabbages."

Mrs. Rose was silent and sorrowful, but not convinced.

The flowers were now closing their petals for
their nightly rest, and the birds were carolling their
vesper hymn. Clarence kissed Mrs. Rose, and bade
her good evening. He then hastened to Linden
Hall.

Mrs. Rose called Biddy to her, and had a consultation, the result of which was, that her faithful servant should leave for the city the next morning, on business of importance.

The result of Harvey's conversation with Clarence was not known, even to his own family, till nearly two years after it took place. It was, however, satisfactory to the persons whom it principally concerned.

Bridget was absent on her journey to the city for several days. During this time, Mrs. Rose employed herself in looking over her trunks and boxes, and making selections of various articles from their multitudinous contents.

She insisted upon taking care of her room, although she said she had never made up a bed before, or swept a room, in her life. Lucy offered to assist her, but was peremptorily refused.

While thus employed she seemed more cheerful than she had been since her arrival at the cottage; the country air and plain wholesome food had entirely restored her to health.

Harvey Amadore called at the cottage the day after his return, and was most cordially received by Mrs. Paverley and Lucy. He asked for Mrs. Rose, and she refused to see him, without assigning any reason.

Various conjectures were made in the family about the object of Bridget's journey, and Mrs.

Rose's occupation in her room. Pete suggested that the lady was going to make them presents, all round, of her nice things, and declared that she probably would give him a pair of yellow kid gloves, like those Clarence wore when he came home to the old brown cottage with his mother.

The mystery was solved when Bridget returned with the big trunk heavier than when she went away.

Mrs. Rose made known her intentions at the tea-table without preamble.

" I am going to be a milliner."

" A milliner ! A milliner ! Where ? " they all exclaimed.

" In the village or town of Hodgton, where I am a perfect stranger. I shall take my maiden name, and, in time, put out my sign — ' Mrs. Truebury, Milliner, from the City.' "

" Mamma, you can't be in earnest," exclaimed Clarence. " What has induced you to form such a plan ? "

" I have my reasons, and will tell them another time to Mrs. Paverley. But you must see the caps and bonnets I have made while you were all wondering what I was about. I always had a turn for making *tasty* caps and other pretty things, and I have made some sweet ones now. You shall see them."

" But you can't set up a millinery, marm, on two

bonnets and three caps," said Pete. " The milliner, who has just got married, and left her shop, had lots and lots of bonnets, caps, and what-nots."

" Left her shop, did you say?"

" Yes, marm, it's just next to the post-office, in Hodgton, and I noticed, yesterday, that it had a board on the front door with ' To Let ' upon it."

" Now, that is just what I want — how lucky! Why, Pete, you see everything that is going on, in town and country."

" Yes, marm, I generally keep my eyes open when I'm awake."

Mrs. Rose asked Mrs. Paverley and Lucy to go to her room, and see the caps and bonnets. They were surprised to see how skilfully and tastefully they were made.

" I always have put away the pieces of silk and lace left over from my dresses ; and now, you see, they have come to use. I little thought what I was saving them for."

Here Mrs. Rose opened the trunk Bridget had taken to the city, and from a number of other articles took out a pattern of mousseline de laine for a dress, and handed it to Mrs. Paverley, and then another for Lucy.

" Please accept these trifles," said she.

Mrs. Paverley and Lucy were too much surprised for a moment even to express their thanks.

" You are quite astonished," said Mrs. Rose, delighted with having produced so lively a sensation. " You need not be afraid to accept my poor gifts. They are paid for. You must know I had an idol, that I cherished proudly and fondly. I gave up a great many things, but the idol I had long wor-shipped I could not sacrifice. But I was severely taunted with my dependence upon others; and I saw those, on whom I was said to be dependent, working, cheerfully, from day to day — cheerfully and constantly. Then a thought came into my head, — I can't tell just what put it there, — if I were to sell my idol, I might do a great deal with the money it would bring. Then another thought came — I might, instead of being so miserably lazy, I might work, too So I sent Biddy to the city with my idol — my red Cashmere shawl. It cost eight hundred dollars; and a good friend of mine bought it for six hundred, and with a part of the money purchased my stock of goods to set up with."

Mrs. Rose laughed heartily at the wonder ex-pressed on the countenances of the listeners. There was no bitterness in that hearty, natural laugh.

" I hope you have not done this, Mrs. Rose, be-cause you have thought yourself a burden to us. We have not been so ungrateful as to forget the many years of kindness shown to my boy," said Mrs. Paverley.

" No, no. You have been, all of you, tender

and sweet to me; but I have been seized with a wish to be like the rest of you — independent; and by a slight sacrifice — a sacrifice of pride — I can become so."

Then Mrs. Rose took from the trunk another parcel, saying, —

"Here are two suits of summer clothes, one for Clarence and another for Pete. I hope they will like them. They are very plain and simple."

What a pleasure it was to Mrs. Rose to be able to "give," instead of always to "receive"! How much purer and more satisfactory the enjoyment than that she had felt in wearing the Cashmere shawl!

Lucy and her mother expressed their thanks warmly, and admired the beautiful dresses which had been selected for them by the friend of Mrs. Rose, who was no other than Mrs. Snett, to whom Biddy had been sent by Mrs. Rose. Instead of written directions, Biddy was left to tell the whole story in her own Irish, eloquent way, and her success was complete.

"And now I have a favor to ask of you, Lucy," said Mrs. Rose, as she closed the big trunk. "Will you take me in the wagon to Hodgton to-day? I want to look at the milliner's shop, and, if it will suit me, to rent it."

"Certainly. I will with pleasure, if you will consent to ride in our homely vehicle, with old Patchy."

" Now, Lucy, don't mortify me by talking in that way. You must know, in giving up my idol, I subdued my pride ; and I haven't been as happy as I am to-day for many, many years."

As the two were driving into Hodgton, a few hours subsequently to the conversation at the white cottage, Lucy said to her companion, —

" I hope, Mrs. Rose, that you will give your own name, if you find the house in the village suits you."

" Mrs. Truebury is my own name in one sense."

" But Mrs. Rose is your own name in every sense. You will probably have to sign a lease, and it would not hold in law if you did not sign your true name." .

" Well, I see I must conquer my old enemy entirely. Why, Lucy, pride is like the hydra Clarence used to study about in his classical books — no sooner is one head cut off than another appears. I will give my own name."

The house and shop exactly suited Mrs. Rose. She called it a " genteel establishment ; " for, besides the shop, there was a nice back parlor, a small dining-room, kitchen on the first floor, and three bedrooms on the second floor. It was hired for one hundred dollars a year.

Mrs. Rose took the reins in her hand to drive Patchy home, quite astonishing Lucy by the overflow of joy, and calling herself a happy woman.

Biddy, of course, went with her to the milliner's

establishment; and another woman was hired to take the place she had recently filled, as assistant dairy-woman at the white cottage.

CHAPTER XXXII.

THE YOUNG TRAVELLER.

WE now pass over two whole years, during which the tenants of the white cottage went on prosperously.

Mrs. Rose became a "fashionable" milliner; but, more than that, she found a pleasure in being useful and in doing good. Her pride and selfishness were subdued, in a great measure, by higher and nobler motives than had before actuated her conduct. Clarence was a frequent visitor, and encouraged her in all her efforts for self-improvement by his own example.

The time had come when he could communicate the proposition made to him by Harvey Amadore from Mr. Fenton, two years previously.

Through Harvey, Mr. Fenton proposed to Clarence, at that time, to go to Europe to learn the arts of landscape gardening and architecture, and he, Mr. Fenton, would furnish the means, saying, like

Hercules, "I am willing to help him who helps himself."

Clarence declined the generous offer, and wrote to Mr. Fenton his reasons, as follows : —

"I am not prepared to go abroad yet. I have not firmness of character, and might easily be led astray. I would like to prepare myself by classical studies and acquiring the French language, and, if possible, German and Italian. I think, with the blessing of health, I might accomplish all this in two years. Besides, I would like to learn from books, to which I can have access in this country, more about landscape gardening and architecture. The latter art I have studied already in the books you, sir, were so kind as to give me, so that I have a technical knowledge of it. England is the place to learn landscape gardening. If, after two years, you think best, sir, to renew your very generous offer, I will (D. V.) accept it most gratefully."

During these two years, Clarence had not neglected his employment as a gardener ; but his one hour of study at noon, daily, and his evening application, especially during the long winter evenings, had enabled him to accomplish what he had proposed to do. Lucy was the companion of his evening studies, and Harvey loaned him the books he needed, and, besides, gave him occasional assistance when he met with difficulties in the languages.

And now, Clarence announced to the family at the white cottage, and to Mrs. Rose, who was taking tea there, that he was about to take a voyage to Europe.

"To Europe!" they exclaimed with one voice.

When Clarence explained the matter, free consent was given.

Immediate preparations were made, and in a week after the announcement Clarence started for New York with Pete, whose first visit was now to be made to the city.

Clarence had written to Mr. Fenton his present wishes, and a cordial, ready answer was returned, inviting him and his brother to pass a few days in New York before he sailed for Europe.

As Clarence and Pete were walking up Broadway, Pete said, "I suppose I should be taken for a country gawky if I look in at these windows; but as I don't know the folks I don't care. Here's a window full of pictures; let's stop a minute to look at them."

They did so; and while wondering and admiring (for it was one of Church's glorious paintings), some one tapped Clarence on the shoulder, and said, in a contemptuous tone, "Clarenth Wothe."

Clarence turned suddenly, and there was his school-day enemy, Stackpole Clap.

"How are you, Stackpole? or Mr. Clap, I should say. This is my brother, Peter, whom, I think, you have seen before;" and a meaning smile lurked about the mouth of Clarence.

"He never *saw* me before unless it was through a hard shower," said Pete, with a loud laugh, which attracted attention from the crowd of gazers at the window.

"Do you mean to insult me, sir?" said Stackpole.

"Just as you choose to take it," was the reply.

Stackpole's slight figure was bent with cringing; he could not stand upright physically, or morally. He looked at Pete, whose stalwart, well-knit person — six feet and one inch tall — was quite alarming, and the determined air with which Pete faced him was not at all agreeable. So Stackpole thought it best to crawl off.

"Don't make a disturbance, Pete," whispered Clarence, imploringly; "you see a crowd is gathering at the prospect of a row, and a policeman is looking on."

"Don't trouble yourself. I should as soon think of meddling with a toad as with that sneak, unless I had a bucket of water to give him a shower-bath."

"I wish you had," said a middle-aged man who was passing at the moment, "for he is the meanest pettifogger in the city, always *swooping* round to find or to make a quarrel."

"That he is," said the policeman. "If any dirty

law business is to be done, Clap is the scamp to do it. He is despised by every honorable man in the profession."

" Come, Pete," said Clarence, walking off; " we are attracting too much attention. We won't stop at any more shop-windows. I thought you were entirely cured of your former *fightiness.*"

" Fightiness do you call it? When I see such a crawling, despicable fellow as that Clap, I long to put my foot upon him as I would upon a centiped," replied Pete, his lip curling with fierce contempt.

" You had better restrain yourself; for in the city you may meet with many such contemptible creatures."

" I don't believe there is but one Stackpole Clap in the world, any more than there is another Quilp like Dickens's Quilp. They are human monsters."

" Well, don't look so angry, Pete; for here we are at Mr. Fenton's door."

Mr. Fenton received Clarence and his brother warmly.

" You have grown famously during these last years," said he to the former, " but your brother has the advantage in height."

" I am five feet eleven and a half; only wanting an inch and a half of Pete's measure," replied Clarence, straightening himself up to his full size.

" You've come just in the right time for dinner;

I have often wished for your company, at my solitary table, Clarence," said Mr. Fenton, as he led the way to the dining-room.

Retiring, as formerly, to the library after dinner, *Mr. Fenton had much to say to Clarence, while Pete surveyed the apartment with curious eyes, and then, at Mr. Fenton's suggestion, examined the engravings and paintings which ornamented it.

After having given Clarence all the needed information with regard to the voyage, and what he was to learn by going abroad, Mr. Fenton turned to Pete, who was carefully scrutinizing a group of cattle by Paul Potter.

"You seem attracted by that picture."

"It's a capital one to my eye, only the horns are too long for my notion; but, after all, there isn't a creature there as handsome as my Pet. I raised her, sir, from a calf, and she's a perfect beauty. I wish I had her picture painted as well as that is."

"You are a good judge; that is considered a remarkable painting. And how do you like the one below it — the sheep in a meadow?"

"In a meadow!" exclaimed Pete, laughing; "we never put sheep in a meadow; and only look at the white-weed and wild flowers of all sorts! Why, sir, sheep eat out all the weeds; the man who painted that picture didn't know the nature of the animals, or he wouldn't have placed them in a meadow."

" Well, the sheep themselves — what do you think of them?"

" They are fancy sheep. Neither south-downs, merinos, black-legs, nor common sheep. The wool is not wool; it's raw cotton. Their faces are human faces entirely. Our sheep often look at me with knowing faces; but still they are sheepish. I've seen men who looked exactly like some of these sheep. I saw one to-day who looked very much like that one, only he had a monkey expression. His name is Clap."

Mr. Fenton was not displeased with Pete's criticism; moreover, he was pleased with Pete's frank, candid manner, although it bordered on bluntness. Meanwhile Clarence listened anxiously to the conversation. He was warmly attached to his brother, and wished him to appear to the best advantage.

" I suppose, Peter, you intend to go to Barnum's Museum. You will see there some strange living animals, human and otherwise."

" The very place I mean to go to right off."

" Take care of your porte-monnaie," said Mr. Fenton, with a mischievous glance at Clarence. " I have heard that country boys' have had their pockets picked at Barnum's."

" O, I am not so green as Clarence was at the time you refer to : my pockets are not worth picking; for my money, what there is of it, isn't there."

So Pete found his way to Barnum's, and Clarence spent the evening with Mr. Fenton.

After two days passed very pleasantly in the city, Clarence sailed in the Africa for Liverpool, and Pete returned home, having seen enough to talk about there for months after.

———◆———

CHAPTER XXXIII.

FIGHTING FORMAN.

AFTER a voyage of eleven days Clarence arrived safely in Liverpool. Glad was he to be once more on *terra firma.* Half the way across the ocean, he would have been *almost* willing to be thrown overboard. At least, he thought he was quite willing to change seasickness to drowning in the sea, to be rid of that horrible nausea. But being once safe on shore, he "thanked God and took courage." Having seen all the objects of interest in Liverpool and its vicinity, to which his guide-book directed him, he took the railway for London, and was whizzed on to that wonder of the modern world, proud London.

As Clarence was walking through one of the narrow streets of London, he was suddenly joined by a man who had been for some time following him with rapid steps.

" You walk fast," said the stranger, a very rough, shabbily dressed man, with dark whiskers and mustache, and heavy frowning eyebrows, wearing green spectacles.

Clarence supposed that the intention of the man must be to rob him; so he quickened his walk almost to a run. His unwelcome companion kept pace with him, step by step.

" So you don't like my company," said he.

" I do not."

" What are you doing here in London?" he roughly said.

" That is no concern of yours."

" But what if I choose to make it my concern?"

Clarence now thought this might be one of the police; but a second thought, as he looked at the dirty, mean dress of his companion, convinced him that was a mistake. He now turned into a more frequented street; but still the stranger walked on with him, now and then laughing in a provoking manner as he peered into Clarence's face, which, with rapid walking and indignation, was as red as the reddest of Englishmen.

" So, then, you won't acknowledge my acquaintance, Mr. Poverty," said the stranger, with a provoking sneer.

" That is not my name; you are mistaken in the person."

" It is your name, with only the change of a letter to suit your circumstanċes to a T."

" You would oblige me by leaving me."

" I couldn't, possibly, till it suits my convenience."

They were now near Craven Street, where Clarence had taken his lodgings.

" So you do not acknowledge the name of Poverty," exclaimed the stranger, with one of his horselaughs.

" My name is Paverley ; there is no disgrace in a name, nor in poverty, but there is in crime and rascality, whatever the name or station of a person may be."

" Even if that name should be the sweet one, the pretty one, Clarenth Wothe." Another startling " haw, haw, haw ! " from the stranger.

Clarence looked at the man eagerly, without the slightest conjecture where he had ever seen him before.

He had now arrived at his lodgings, and as he rang at the door, the fellow looked at the number, and then, making a low bow, said, —

" Mr. Clarenth Wothe Poverty, I will see you again," and walked rapidly away, leaving Clarence much disturbed, and not a little alarmed.

Craven Street. The very street in which Franklin lodged when he was in London a century ago ! Perhaps, for that reason, Clarence had taken his lodgings there, for Franklin's "Life," written by Sparks, he had more than read; he had carefully studied it. Perhaps he was in the very room the philosopher had occupied; at all events it was a pleasant and a cheering thought. Like Benjamin Franklin, he was making his own way in spite of obstacles; and though he might not become as great and as distinguished as that statesman and philosopher, he might become a useful man. On the evening of that same day, Clarence had letters to write, and remained in his room.

About nine o'clock a servant handed him a soiled card, on which was scrawled " John Jimson, Esq."

Could it be that the stranger was his former schoolmate, Jack Jimson!

It was indeed. Before he could say whether he would receive him or not, Jack pushed aside the servant who stood at the door of Clarence's room, and rushed in.

But in what a plight! His head was bound up with an old red cotton handkerchief, and a torn slouched hat hung partly over his face, which was disfigured by deep scratches, from which blood was still oozing.

Jack threw himself upon the floor, and rolled over and over as though in violent pain.

Clarence looked compassionately at the poor wretch, but could not speak to him.

After a few moments Jack got up and seated

himself in a chair near the table at which Clarence had been writing, and took an impertinent survey of the letter, which Clarence had nearly finished.

" So, then, you wouldn't recognize an old friend when you met him," said Jack.

" I did not know you at all, you are so changed every way."

" Every way ! That's so. I am a six-footer in my stocking feet, when I have any stockings ; and look at that arm. Isn't that a man's arm ! "

Here Jack stripped up his dirty shirt-sleeve, — for he had no coat on, — and showed a brawny arm, with the big muscles as hard as iron.

" There's an arm for you," said the young ruffian, putting that boasted arm into a boxing attitude. " Dolly-boy can't show one like it."

" You are as fond of fighting as ever, I see," said Clarence.

" Why, it's my occupation," replied Jack, with a coarse laugh ; " have you a better one, my pretty boy ? "

" I am sorry you have so poor a one ! "

" A very good one in England. You have heard of the gentlemen of the fancy. Why, man ! I'm the best boxer in the country."

" How came you here, Jack ? I have never heard a word of you since Christmas day, nearly four years since."

" O, I remember ; I saw you last when I was

with Stackpole on a sleigh-ride. Well, father shut me up for that spree. I got out the window, and ran away. I shipped as a common sailor on board a vessel bound for Liverpool, and I have been living in England by hook and by crook ever since. Now I'm short of money, and want to borrow. Can you lend me five pounds, that is, twenty-five dollars in Yankee currency?"

" I cannot. I have been sent to England for a special purpose by a friend of mine, and have no money of my own."

" O, ho! You are Harvey Amadore's servant, then. I'm sorry for you. He is as proud as he is mean, and as mean as he is proud."

" He is my best friend, and I will not hear him abused," replied Clarence, warmly.

Jack Jimson started from the chair, doubled up his big fists, and exclaimed, " How are you going to help it?" and then he brought one of those big fists in close contact with the side of Clarence's head, without striking him.

" Now, Jack, listen to me," said Clarence, without moving an inch. " Do you want to go home? If I should lend you the money, and pay it myself to Harvey Amadore, would you return to your parents?"

" As a prodigal son, I suppose you mean. No, indeed! I have no such intention; but I do intend to have the money; so out with it at once, or I'll take it *sans cérémonie.*"

Just as Jack uttered the last word, a loud tramping was heard on the stairs, and soon a violent knocking at the door of Clarence's room.

Jack crawled under the bed. Clarence opened the door. Two powerful-looking watchmen demanded " Fighting Forman," who had been traced to that room.

Clarence turned his eyes towards the bed to see if Jack was entirely concealed.

The watchmen understood it as an indication that he was there, and both the men sprang to the spot, and, in spite of Jack's resistance, dragged him out, and with a strong rope tied his hands behind him. Clarence, who had not spoken a word, looked on in utter amazement.

When Jack was fairly mastered and entirely under the control of the watchmen, Clarence asked what the man (Jack) had been doing, and why they handled him so roughly.

" It's very likely you know. You must be one of his gang."

Jack's laugh at this was perfectly demoniac.

" We have no order to arrest you," continued the man, " but we shall keep a close eye upon you."

" I am a citizen of the United States, and only arrived in London day before yesterday. Here is my passport, my letter of credit on the house of Peabody & Co., and my letter of introduction to our ambassador."

" The watchmen dragged him out and tied his hands behind him."

Page 234.

Clarence drew the letters from his pocket as he spoke, and, at the same time, the landlord of the house testified that his lodger came there recommended by a gentleman in the city.

" Then how came Fighting Forman to take refuge here after knocking down two of the watchmen?" inquired the first speaker.

" He came for money. He happened to have known me in the United States. He is a citizen of the Union."

" Very likely. Come along, villain. The gallows is too good for you. You meant to have committed robbery, too."

Jack, during all this time, had maintained a sullen silence. Now he said, with an oath, " I am not a Yankee."

As they led him off, he turned to Clarence with a hideous grin, and, shaking his fist in the face of Clarence, said, —

" If I had only had two minutes more, I should have had the money and been off safely. Another chance will offer, and you shan't crow over me then, you mean, low-spirited Yankee."

" I pity you ; from the bottom of my heart I pity you," said Clarence, with deep feeling.

" I despise your pity ! " exclaimed Jack, with a terrible oath, as the watchmen dragged the miserable wretch down stairs to place him in the watchhouse for the night, and then to bring him before the police court in the morning.

"So, then," thought Clarence, "this is what Bully Jimson has come to through his love of fighting and his propensity to all kinds of wickedness. What a lesson! God be thanked that I have been kept from such horrible crimes. To disclaim his country, too! A lying traitor! Well, his country would be disgraced if he acknowledged himself a citizen. I will leave him to his fate. Perhaps it will be imprisonment for life, or even hanging."

Indeed, so it proved; for one of the watchmen whom Jack knocked down was killed by the blow, and Bully Jimson's life ended on the gallows.

CHAPTER XXXIV.

NEWS FROM HOME.

AFTER having visited many of the beautiful country-seats of the nobility and gentry of England, Clarence went to Scotland, and there remained for a few months, at Sandy's earnest entreaty, to learn something of practical gardening. From thence he went to the Continent, and saw France and Italy more thoroughly than most travellers. He then returned to London, and placed himself in the studio of an architect and landscape gardener.

Not many months after his return to England, he received the following letter from Harvey Amadore : —

THE LINDENS.

MY DEAR CLARENCE : Before this meets your eye, you must have learned from the newspapers, that our beloved country is racked to its very foundation. Ambitious politicians at the south are leading the slave-holding people on to their ruin.

You must have heard of the attack upon Fort Sumter in South Carolina — South Carolina, the leader in rebellion.

I will not recapitulate what has already become history. All Europe will be looking on, with eager expectation, to the result of this fearful contest. Every man who loves his country ought to be at home at this eventful period.

You will be surprised to learn that Harvey Amadore is now *Captain* Amadore. I am raising a volunteer company, and, at my own expense, arming and equipping the soldiers. Your brother Peter is my color-sergeant, and a noble-looking fellow is he, as he proudly lifts the glorious stars and stripes. I think, however, that as the company will choose some of their officers, he may go as second lieutenant.

I am sorry to call you away from your artistic pursuits ; but everything else must give way at this time for the good of our country. Mr. Fenton requested me to write to you, and say that you have his consent to return. Indeed, he says it is a disgrace for a citizen of the United States to remain abroad when he may be of service at home.

Whenever my company leaves for the army, you, my dear Clarence, will have to look after my affairs at Linden Hill, and to take charge of your mother and sister.

Mrs. Rose, too, is anxious for your return. She is wonderfully patriotic, and wears the red, white, and blue, in all possible ways in which these colors can appear in woman's attire.

My time is much occupied, for we drill twice a day. Besides studying military tactics myself, I employ an able drill-master, at present; and I think, whenever we join a regiment, we shall not be a discreditable addition.

It is worth living for to see a people, as with one heart and soul, uniting enthusiastically to put down rebellion. With God's aid it will be done.

Excuse this hasty, disconnected scrawl. I trust we shall soon meet, and discuss these weighty matters more at leisure.

I suppose you will take the very next steamer that leaves, after the reception of this letter.

Truly yours,
HARVEY AMADORE.

Clarence immediately prepared to leave England with a saddened heart, but full of ardor and love for his native land. His residence and travels in foreign countries had made him only the more sensible of the blessings of a free government. And that a maddened, Satan-led portion of that country, should attempt to break up and destroy such a government, seemed to him as incredible as if three or four of the planets should attempt to destroy the solar system, or to separate themselves from it.

Only three days after the reception of the letter from Captain Amadore, Clarence was taking his last look of England from the deck of the steamer.

CHAPTER XXXV.

CAPTAIN AMADORE.

THE very day on which Clarence arrived home was the one on which the company of Captain Amadore, numbering one hundred and one, was about to leave to join the —— Regiment of New York Volunteers. It was just before sunset on the 4th of July. Already, with knapsacks on their backs, their canteens filled, and their arms brightly gleaming, they were assembled on the green of Hodgton. A crowd of weeping women and children were looking on. For half an hour the soldiers were dismissed to take a last leave of these sorrowing, yet rejoicing friends. Rejoicing, for such were the zeal and patriotism of the women, that they gave up to their country what was most precious to them, although the sacrifice was a heart-rending one.

Clarence soon found his mother and Lucy among the crowd, and was welcomed by them with a burst of tears — joy and thankfulness mingling with their sorrow, just as the sun's rays at that moment mingled with a sudden shower, and a beautiful rainbow spanned the eastern sky.

Lucy pointed to the auspicious banner in the heavens, and whispered, " Hope."

Pete, in his regimentals, with the lieutenant's strap on his shoulder, stepped up proudly to Clarence, and gave him such a grip of the hand as almost to cause a shriek.

" Why, old fellow, you are magnificent," said Clarence. " I thought you were color-sergeant? "

" I should have liked to have carried the stars and stripes to the war, but the captain wanted me for his second lieutenant, and I obey captain's orders, whatever they may be."

Evidently the tall soldier was choking down his feelings, while he spoke to Clarence ; but when he turned to his mother and Lucy, the manly lieutenant could no longer control them. Big tears, which he indignantly shook off, betrayed what he considered unmanly weakness.

Harvey came to greet Clarence, and took him aside to give him some directions with regard to the management at Linden Hill, during the captain's absence.

"You know," said he, "that poor Sandy is at rest."

"At rest!"

"Gone to his long home. Better for him, no doubt, than to have been left in his old age to mourn over the condition of his adopted country. You will now have the sole charge of the garden and grounds, as master. Employ as many workmen as you please. The head work is all that will be required of you."

After a few parting words with Mrs. Paverley and Lucy, Harvey put himself at the head of his company. The band struck up Yankee Doodle, as if to drown sorrow and excite patriotic enthusiasm by that lively air; and the Hodgton company marched away, followed by the earnest prayers of mothers, wives, sisters, and sweethearts.

"Ah, few shall *meet*, where many *part*," for the battle-field will be their death-bed, and their requiem the cannon's roar.

When the Paverley family returned home to the white cottage, they could give the cordial welcome to Clarence, which their absorbed interest in the company had prevented. Mrs. Rose was with them; a long ribbon of red, white, and blue was

16

worn on one arm, and.her bonnet was trimmed with the same colors. These outward demonstrations of patriotism were true to the fervent sentiment within the bosom of Mrs. Rose. Night and day she had worked for the soldiers, scraping lint, rolling bandages, and making " Havelocks."

Mrs. Rose had been prosperous in her business, and was now aided in her work by two apprentices. Her joy at the return of Clarence was almost as great as if he had indeed been her own son.

" Who would have thought that you were to become an artist?" said she, regarding Clarence with intense admiration. " A landscape gardener and architect! That sounds well." And then she whispered to Lucy, " Isn't he splendid ! "

Though very differently expressed, even deeper was the joy of Mrs. Paverley and Lucy.

During the absence of Clarence, his sister had kept on with her studies and a course of reading on the countries he was visiting, aided by books from Captain Amadore's library, till she was almost as familiar with the cathedrals of England, and the ancient remains of art in Italy, as Clarence himself. It became, in time, a source of intense pleasure to the brother and sister to " compare notes " on these subjects.

The dreadful storm of war swept over the land like a tornado, felling to the earth alike the fresh, young hopes of home and country, and the stout, stern men of riper years.

Scarcely ten months elapsed before Harvey was desperately wounded while gallantly leading on a part of the regiment to which he was attached. Pete had become first lieutenant of the company. No braver soldier was in that regiment than Peter Paverley; and now he was captain of the company which had been raised by Harvey. In the battle in which Harvey lost an arm and was wounded in the knee, his life was saved by Peter; the brave lieutenant struck down with his sword a rebel, who stooped over the wounded captain to despatch him with a bowie-knife.

Peter then, with the aid of a soldier, gently placed Harvey on a stretcher, and he was carried to the rear. When the battle had been fought and won by our gallant army, Harvey was carried to a hospital, where his right arm was amputated, and a bullet extracted from his knee. There, in the hospital, he remained for three months, vibrating between life and death. Nothing but his calm, resigned state of mind, and the strict temperance of his former life, which had kept his blood pure, saved him (humanly speaking), from the grasp of death. One of the devoted women who attended most lovingly to the wounded in that hospital, remarked, " that of all the patients she had seen, Captain Amadore was the most cheerful." And when she lamented that he should have lost an arm, his reply was, " I couldn't have lost it in a better cause ; and I trust God has saved my life that I may witness the final success of this struggle, and the restoration of my country to unity and peace."

After an absence of more than a year from home, Harvey returned to the Lindens.

The house had been closed, and Aunty Dotty was living with another relative many miles distant. It was a desolate abode for one still feeble from long and dangerous illness. The servant who had attended Captain Amadore ever since he left home alone was with him now. As soon as Clarence heard of Harvey's arrival, he hastened to him with intense interest and sympathy. Harvey was reclining, pale and languid, on a sofa in the library. At the sight of Clarence he raised himself, and extended his left hand. A bright smile illumined his pale countenance, as he gave Clarence a cordial greeting.

Alas! Clarence could only see that loose, empty coat-sleeve, and the thin, wasted form which had gone forth so full of manly strength and beauty. Tears filled his eyes, and a silent grasp of the hand, the only hand, testified his grief.

"Cheer up, man; don't look so doleful. I shall soon get back my health in this sweet country air. How lovely the old place looks! As I drove up the avenue, I was struck with the great improvement you have made in it during my absence."

"Thank you," said Clarence, with a husky voice.

" And how are Mrs. Paverley, and Miss Lucy, and Mrs. Rose, too. Are they all as patriotic as ever?"

" Even more so."

" Well, they will have one soldier at home to care for, who will not, however, prevent them from more extended benevolence. Now, Clarence, I have been thinking there is no nurse who would suit me as well as your good mother. Can you persuade her to leave the white cottage and come to the Lindens, with Miss Lucy and yourself, till I am stronger?"

" If you wish it, certainly."

" Well, then, please make your arrangements as speedily as possible. Take your choice of the rooms in this dreary house, and drive out the rats, who have taken full possession."

It was with reluctance that the Paverley family left the white cottage, where they had passed so many quiet, pleasant years in contented labor.

Mrs. Rose said she could spare Biddy to take charge of the dairy and poultry-yard till the family returned to the cottage; and so they flitted to the Lindens without removing an article, excepting wearing apparel.

Good Mrs. Paverley! Sad, indeed, it was to her as she took the place beside the sofa of Captain Amadore, to feed him almost as she would a child; for he had not yet acquired facility in the use of his left hand. The wound in his knee had injured the joint, so that he was quite lame. And yet withal he was so cheerful! When he saw the tears streaming over Mrs. Paverley's cheek, he said, —

"Don't weep for me, Mrs. Paverley. It is God's will. Besides, there are many poor fellows in a much worse condition than I am. I hope the country will take care of those who haven't a home of their own."

The mother's thoughts now went forth to her own absent son, and her hand so trembled that she could scarcely carry the spoon, with which she was giving soup to her patient, to his mouth.

Clarence was so much occupied with new cares and duties, in addition to those which had previously devolved upon him, that he had very little time to spare to Harvey.

Day by day the invalid was gaining strength. After he had been at home nearly a fortnight, he said to Clarence, —

"Do you know my eyes are so weak that I cannot read without pain?"

"Is it possible! Cannot Moses read to you?"

Moses was the captain's servant.

Harvey laughed as he replied, "His reading is à la Partington. The other day, in attempting to give me the news from a paper, he read, 'variable institution without ammunition.' Now, what do you suppose it really was?"

" I can't conjecture."

" Valuable information without remuneration."

" Lucy is a good reader ; she might assist you."

" If she would be so obliging it would be a great favor. I am anxious for my daily paper, and when it comes it is tantalizing, for I cannot read a column without pain."

Now Lucy had not seen the captain since his return ; and as there were servants in the house to attend to the work of the family, she had been comparatively idle.

When Clarence proposed that she should become Harvey's reader, she expressed diffidence as to her ability ; but Clarence reassured her, and she, at last, consented to go to the library, at eleven o'clock daily, to read the paper.

Clarence had not done justice to Lucy in saying she was " a good reader : " she was more. Her voice was one of uncommon sweetness and compass. Its modulations and cadences were charming ; there was always in it an under-current of pathos. Moreover, she was an appreciative reader, and gave emphasis and expression to every sentence. From reading the newspaper, Lucy was persuaded to read favorite books from the library, while Mrs. Paverley sat by with her knitting — her favorite employment, now devoted to soldiers' stockings.

Thus passed many pleasant hours. Harvey was able, after some weeks, to hobble about with the aid of a cane, and to use his left hand quite felicitously. He learned rapidly to write with it — a back hand, however; he could not write otherwise.

A little pony carriage was ordered from the city, and in this he could drive about the grounds with Clarence.

It was the rose season, leafy June, when he made his first excursion, and the beauty of the garden was so intensely exciting, that, for the first time since his return, his eyes moistened with tears.

" Clarence," said he, " how wonderful it is that God has given man the ability to improve the Creator's own works. Here must be forty or fifty varieties of roses, all from the original little five-leaved flower."

" Seventy varieties," replied Clarence, proudly, " and a dozen more if my experiments prove successful. And now you must look at your strawberries. There are twenty varieties here."

A hedge of daily roses surrounded the strawberry-beds, which occupied a large space.

" Sweets to the sweet," said Harvey.

Clarence placed the reins in Harvey's hand, and stepped out of the low pony carriage to gather a bunch of the " *triomphe de Gand* " for Harvey, the first strawberries that had ripened. They then drove about the grounds, and over and over again Harvey expressed his delight at the beautiful improvements Clarence had planned and executed.

The next morning after the drive about the grounds, as Lucy was reading the morning paper, she suddenly stopped. The name of Captain Paverley attracted her attention. She read the passage to herself.

"What is it?" inquired Harvey, anxiously.

"O, sir, my brother has been promoted for bravery in the last battle under General Sheridan. He is now Major Paverley."

Harvey took the paper from Lucy, and read the passage.

"In an extreme emergency, Captain Paverley volunteered to pass the river with his company for a reconnoissance. It was an exceedingly dangerous and difficult attempt; but it proved entirely successful, with the loss of only two men killed and five wounded. Captain Paverley, for his remarkable coolness and bravery, was promoted. He now ranks as major. He is one of the bravest and best officers in the —— Regiment of New York Volunteers."

"True, very true; your brother well deserves promotion. You know, Lucy, I owe my life to him, under Providence. Pete is a noble fellow. The boys in the company were very proud of him. God grant he may be spared for his country's sake."

A slight shade of sadness passed over Harvey's usually serene, cheerful countenance, and he added, "I try to be contented to be laid aside like a use-

less old hulk; but when I hear of these daring
deeds my heart throbs and my brain whirls.   I
long for the field."

"Is it possible!" exclaimed Lucy.   "We are all
so thankful to have you here, gradually regaining
your health."

Harvey pointed to his right shoulder and his lame
knee, and sighed.

With a trembling voice Lucy renewed the reading.

Two months had passed, and Captain Amadore
had not entirely regained his health and strength;
but he no longer needed careful nursing.

Mrs. Paverley proposed to return to the white
cottage.

At this proposal Harvey became thoughtful and
sad.

"I shall be very lonely without you and Clarence, and," — here Harvey hesitated, and after a
moment's pause added, "and my excellent reader.
Why need you leave?"

"I think it is time for me to attend to the dairy.
Biddy and her helper have done pretty well, but I
think, sir, it would be more for your interest if I
attended to the business."

"It would be much more for my interest to have
you remain here.   I will speak to Clarence about it."

So, the first opportunity that occurred, Harvey
opened the subject, or, rather in a roundabout way,
came to it.

"Have you thought, Clarence, how and where you are to be established in your profession as architect and landscape gardener?"

"I have not formed any definite plan."

"You have shown your skill here, and I prize you highly; but you ought to be setting up for yourself. For my own pleasure I would retain you near me; but you have talent and taste that will lead you to eminence and usefulness. I shall be most happy to aid you in any possible way in setting up for yourself."

"Thank you, captain. Through your generous kindness, and Mr. Fenton's, I am ready to put out my shingle, as the saying is, in some city. I think I should like Boston. There is more taste for landscape gardening there, I am told, than in any other part of our country, and a need of educated architects. Besides, I like the style of folks there. They are liberal, intellectual, and refined. But I should be sorry to leave you; and now, in Pete's absence, I don't like to leave my mother and sister."

"I will be a son to your mother if she will accept me as such," — the color mounted to the forehead of Harvey as he added, "and more than a brother to your sister."

Clarence was taken by surprise, and looked wistfully at Harvey for explanation.

With some embarrassment, he continued, —

"I feel as though it would be cruel to ask any woman to be my 'other half,' when I could add only a quarter myself; so you see it would be asking three quarters to my fraction in order to make 'one,' scripturally."

This was said with an effort at pleasantry, but the deep under-current of sadness betrayed itself.

Clarence was entirely at a loss what reply to make. Harvey continued, "I have never seen Lucy's equal. Do you think it would be unjust and unkind to your sister to ask her to aid me in making my shattered existence comfortable, and in helping me to be of some use in the world?"

"Neither unjust nor unkind; but I have supposed that other motives ought to actuate a man in such a case. I am not romantic, but I believe in the sentiment that binds two into one."

Harvey laughed a bitter laugh; it was the only tincture of bitterness that had poisoned his heart since his misfortune.

"Then you think I am not capable now of inspiring that sentiment."

"Never were you more worthy. Never were you so truly and nobly manly as now," replied Clarence, warmly and earnestly; then, after a moment's pause, he added, "Harvey, speak to Lucy yourself."

"I have never been alone with her a moment in my life, and, I assure you, had never entertained any other sentiment than that of friendship till since my return home. Her devotion as a daughter and a sister won my esteem. On a nearer acquaintance, I find in her all those attributes calculated to render a quiet, retired country-life agreeable and useful. My only fear is, that she is so compassionate and so disinterested, that she will merely accept my proposals from pity. That I could not endure ; and yet," he added with a sigh, "what other motive could induce her to take charge of such a helpless being as I am?"

"I can only repeat what I have said. Speak to Lucy yourself. You have my best wishes." So saying Clarence left Harvey, and requested Lucy to step into the library.

CHAPTER XXXVI.

WHO WOULD HAVE THOUGHT IT!

Letter from Pete : —

MOTHER, DEAR MOTHER : We are on the eve of a battle. I think it will be a tremendous one. Perhaps I shall share the fate of many a brave fellow, and be left on the battle-field.

Mother, at such a time as this, a man examines himself, to know what he has done and what he has left undone.

I have not been to you all that I ought to have been. Many times I have been wilful and undutiful. I now ask your forgiveness. If I fall in battle, remember me kindly. It nerves me to think you will be praying for me. Of all the blessings God has given me, I thank him most heartily, at this moment, for having given me a good, pious mother and sister.

Give my best love to Lucy and Captain Amadore. I am sorry to learn that he has not recovered the use of that wounded leg, and that he is still very lame. What a mercy it is that he has such a helpmeet and companion as our dear, modest, sweet Lucy! God bless them both.

Clarence, you tell me, is doing well in Boston. Love to him. He has been a true, kind brother to me; more kind than I have been to him. O, how I love you all!

In haste, your devoted son,

PETE.

P. S. Already I hear the distant roar of an attack upon one of our columns. God be with us, and defend the right cause, the cause of truth and justice!

Not many months after the receipt of Pete's letter, the news reached the white cottage of the fall of Richmond and the surrender of Lee's army. Alas for the awful calamity that followed!—a calamity, the sorrow for which will never pass from the hearts of all who loved and honored our truly great and excellent President! Abraham Lincoln's example remains a rich bequest to every boy who would attain to " true manliness."

Pete came home Colonel Paverley.

" Who would have thought it! " exclaimed the delighted mother. " Our Pete a colonel! "

Mrs. Rose was soon at the white cottage to congratulate the colonel on having so well served his country.

" And what are you going to do with yourself now? " she asked. " I suppose you have got so attached to the army, you will not be willing to throw aside your regimentals."

" Indeed, I shall be willing to do so till my country calls me to her aid again," he replied; " but," he added, fervently, " may that time be far distant; or, rather, may we never have cause to defend ourselves again from a foe, domestic or foreign, as long as this great republic endures. I am going back to farming, and expect my good mother to live with me."

" Indeed! Like Cincinnatus and Washington," said Mrs. Rose, " you go back to the plough."

The colonel smiled, as he said, " You place great

examples before me. I have just come from the Lindens. Captain Amadore has leased to me the outlying farm of Hardscrabble. There I expect to employ my skill in farming ; to bring a rough, unproductive soil into a state of high cultivation. My highest ambition is to be a first-rate farmer."

" Well, colonel," said Mrs. Rose, " I have found from experience, that there is nothing so conducive to happiness in this world, as being regularly and constantly employed, in such a way as to be independent yourself, and able and inclined to do good to others, who are not able to help themselves. Clarence has offered to have me come and live with him in Boston, where he is succeeding wonderfully in his profession ; but I have declined his generous offer, for the sake of what poor old Sandy would have called ' the glorious privilege of being independent.'

" Or," said Colonel Paverley, " as one of our own poets hath it, —

'Independent of all, save the mercy of God.'"